Silence
of My
Father

Silence of My Father

Ron Savage

NEW PULP PRESS

For information contact:
Publisher@NewPulpPress.com

ISBN-13: 978-1945734113 (New Pulp Press)
ISBN-10: 1945734116

To my Janny

Silence
of My
Father

And she who is born,
she who sings and cries,
she who begins the passage, her hair
sprouting out,
her gums budding for first spring on earth,
the mist still clinging about
her face, puts
her hand
into her father's mouth, to take hold of
his song.

- Galway Kinnell

@*wren& me1* Hi 2 Wren's fans! Left Chicago 4 Philly. Hospital done, I'm great! But still 2 dark, 2 weird. xxooxx to all!

ONE

BUT WHAT OF the father, the man who is all men? That's what therapists want to know; it's what Dr. Allison will ask me. The night my husband left us – the "us" being our boy Carlos, Jr. and Yours Truly – my son had gone to a sleepover earlier and I was alone and crazy. Carlos, Jr. and I had no tip-off that the family was about to lose a piece of itself. Minutes after that good-bye I'd walked out of our two bedroom apartment in downtown Chicago, rushed across North LaSalle and got slammed by a taxi. Both my right hip and my collarbone had multiple fractures. The ER doctor said I was very lucky but I didn't feel lucky. It took months to heal, the physical therapy, the pain, you don't know. And though I would not start with Dr. Allison for another six months, I shouldn't have to tell you how therapists love connecting a husband leaving his wife and his son to the wife stepping in front of a moving taxi.

But what of the father, the man who is all men? Yes, well. In three or four days the movers came to gather my husband's things. Our apartment looked unbelievably empty, devastatingly empty. About that time I began to obsess about my father, a man who'd also left his family. I had been very young then. And a statistic, I was one of five million kids being raised by a single parent, my mother. In another ten years I'd be one of fifteen million. And so on and so on. After my husband left, I began thinking about my father, dreaming about him, and weeping. Don't get me wrong, I missed Carlos, Sr. But I wept for my father.

I DON'T KNOW if the following story is true or one I invented or a story Mother told me. There are many doubtful stories like this in my life. Mother says my father was English. They met in London during the summer months and she was still an undergrad from Temple U. He was a boy from Manchester, she says. A beautiful boy. Who knows for sure, I don't. Reality isn't a clear thing with us. Perhaps that's not true with most. I think most people trust their history. With Mother and me, "what was" always has been a mix of history and lies.

It begins with my father laying in the desert, his left leg shredded and bloody at the knee and down the calf. The leg doesn't hurt much at first but five or ten minutes later it starts burning him. Then it burns him so much he faints. Soon my father doesn't know the number of times he has gone in and out of consciousness. He faints and wakes and faints again. Blood is soaking his khakis, soaking the sand and the red brittle clay under his leg. He looks for shade, a tree to spread its shadow over him. The air from the sun is too hot to breathe; it hurts his throat, the inside of his nose. But he couldn't move to a shady tree if he saw one.

Birds watch him, nine and counting. This is up from the two or three that began the day. *You can't hide a good meal.* These are big hideous birds with scarlet faces and white beaks and wide black wings. One bird is gliding overhead, circling on the current. Some have become brave and very impatient. They're walking toward him, menacing, nonchalant – old shuffling men in black suits. He tosses handfuls of sand to keep them at a distance. But the wind is strong and it blows the sand back at him. Wind shows the underside of dark feathers. He can also smell the birds, the stink of what they have been eating. Or maybe it's the stink of his own leg. A new bird has settled-in and starts to bob its head and pace. The others get vocal and thrash the sand with their wings to scare it off. But the new bird is hungry like the others and refuses to go.

MY FATHER traveled to the Sinai Peninsula in 1973, the Yom Kipper War. He had photographed the Egyptian army crossing the Suez. He was a photojournalist who sold pictures to the TV network and the newspaper who'd give him the best price.

"You can make a very nice dollar in the war." That was what he once said to mother. "Sure it's dangerous. Hey a lot of things are dangerous. Am I right? But you stay quicker than them, you stay smarter." Life was about taking chances but the right chances, that's what my father thought.

His buyers were from Europe, America and the Middle East, people praised his work. The networks and the newspapers liked putting their words to his photographs and one photograph could tell many different stories. Photographs are flexible things.

A young Egyptian soldier with a machine gun had fired on my father from the top of a tank. The soldier first said something in Arabic and father held up his prized Nikon F Photomic FTN. "Sahibi, sahibi!" my father shouted and waved the camera at the man. *Friend, friend!*

But the soldier was wired for war and didn't trust the accent. This is what Mother believes. It's never anything personal. War simply has a way of preparing the men andwomen who are about to jump into it.

Tat-tat-tat-tat-tat.

The noise was playful, quieter than expected, a

sandy line kicked up toward our photojournalist. It went halfway up his left leg. Bits of flesh and khaki fanned out with the blood. My father felt his legs wilt and vanish beneath him but he didn't remember collapsing onto the sand. What he did remember was the roar and tremble of the tank rolling by him.

ONE OF THE birds gets too close and Father grabs its skinny neck and surprises himself. He probably also surprised the bird. *Okay now the fuck what?* He's too weak for this. But letting the bird go isn't a good idea. The thing is screeching and going nuts. Its black wings are enormous and the wings beat down on him and its talons cut into his bicep. Other birds begin screeching. One or two perch on higher rocks. Most hop away from the fuss, big wings beating, a squall of sand whipping about their feathers, the sand partially hiding them.

The talons cut my father for a second time and he slaps the bird hard on the side of its red face. *Do to me, I do to you.* It's automatic, it's satisfying. He hears the neck crack and the bird suddenly drops in his fist. It dangles there, dead, heavy. And that is that. He's more surprised by killing the ugly thing than grabbing it. Father can't believe this. He looks around, hoping someone might be there to share his triumph. How he got tough with a bird.

The burn has come back. It's not too bad now but it will get worse. It'll burn the way a pig on a spit burns. A BBQ burn. Once the burn starts it won't stop until he faints. Thinking about fainting is terrifying to him until he goes out. Then it's a blessing. But since he is out it's only a blessing other people know. This was one of my father's beliefs. Fainting is what he thought of when he thought of death. No heaven, no hell. Folks just "go out" and other folks say, "What a blessing he didn't suffer."

Who's going to save my ass? This bothers him more than the young soldier who shot him, more than the burn or the very real possibility of fainting. *Where is my luck when I need it?* That's what he's thinking, what he wants to know – at least according to Mother. Where are the good cards, the good roll of the dice? Isn't it that straightforward, that precarious? It's all about being in the right or wrong place at the right or wrong time. *Who's going to save me from these damn birds?*

LITTLE BABY RHEA, he'd called me. And it's been thirty-five or six years since last I saw him. I have photos, of course, and I remember things, his lime cologne, the smell of the cigarettes he smoked. Or I *think* I do, just don't ask me to swear to it. The photos show him as a tall and slender man with brushed back tan-brown hair that was thick and unquestionably difficult to comb. His eyes were – or maybe *are* – dark, large and disarming.

Most of Mother's bedtime stories had to do with my father and me.

"Tell me about the zoo," I'd say. Such an enabler.

Our family lived in Philadelphia and Daddy and his darling little Rhea liked going

to the zoo on the bank of the Schuylkill. There were shade trees and the sunlight drifted between the thick branches and the leaves. Vendors sold popcorn and roasted peanuts in paper bags. They sold soft pretzels that were warm and very salty and squirted with wavy thin lines of mustard.

"Your daddy knew all about the animals," my mother said.

"And he'd always buy me a pretzel."

"Yes, you loved your pretzels."

"And we'd hold hands."

"Well he loved you very much and didn't want you getting lost. The zoo is a terribly big place. Lots of trees and pathways, you remember that."

"I guess so." I was never positive about it.

"How about the accent? Do you remember his English accent? You loved his accent. My Rhea always wanted Daddy to read her bedtime stories. 'Talk more,' you'd tell him. Remember?"

"...sort of." I did remember the accent. Or perhaps Mother had talked enough about it over the years for it to seem familiar.

Most people enjoy and trust their memories the way they enjoy, say, an old song or a movie like *Casablanca*. But when we have so little to go on, we embellish, don't we? Most of us fill in the spaces, add a logical detail here and there, give the devil a little more bite. We should never think children are reliable and wise. Children are children and we can love them for being who they are without getting caught in their fantasies. I don't have faith in what I recall so early in my life but what else is there to go on?

Jeffery David Waye, that was my father's name – *is* his name.

J.D. Waye.

Oh I don't think he's alive now. No, no, I don't. But a part of me has never given him up. I'm always on the look out, so-to-speak. I imagine him appearing one day, *poof!* like that. Maybe he will sweep me into his arms and put his rough cheek to mine and tell me how sorry he is for going away and how he will never do such a scary and awful thing again.

MY FATHER TRIES to throw the dead bird at the other birds but he is too weak to do the job and the dead bird skids across the ground, bumping over small rocks and bits of grass, raking up the sand. Father's torn and bloody leg gets jostled in the toss and the burn is upped a notch and makes itself known. His leg doesn't like being stretched or moved or messed with. *Please don't let me faint now.*

The afternoon heat is powerful and the air ripples in a cloudless and brilliant sky. As the dead bird slides toward the other birds, they squawk and screech and hop away. Some take to the air; some go to a safer piece of ground. It's the new bird who stays put and watches. It's the new one who won't be intimidated.

"Don't look at me with those eyes," Father says. Golden eyes, that's what he told Mother.

The bird cocks his head and blinks. "I'm nobody's meal." This said to remind himself. The new bird spreads and flutters its black wings then settles down again. He is not a deep thinker. None of them are deep thinkers. But they know there is something not far from them with meat on it. And when that thing stops moving and stops making noise, they will go in and take the meat and let the sun have the bones.

THIS WAS ONE of Mother's favorite stories. Notice how she leaves my father hanging there. No rain, no shade, no cigarettes and definitely no rescue. Just the birds getting closer. *Is the buffet ready now?* Every-so-often she'd let me have an honest look at her anger. My father lingered perpetually on the edge of hell and with no forgiveness. It was her version of Dante's *Divine Comedy*. It's the last part of the William Congreve poem.

Yes, thou shalt know, spite of thy past Distress,
And all those ills which thou so long has mourn'd;
Heav'n has no Rage, like love to Hatred turn'd,
Nor Hell a Fury, like a Woman scorn'd.

I did not think about the meaning of things until

my early or mid-teens. But at age eleven I began to illustrate some of the images from her stories, what I'd imagined the images might be. And I liked the desert story very much. I would sit in the pine rocker by our big living room window, a wood bread board on my lap to support my art tablet. I always worked quickly but with an eye for symmetry and detail. Even then I had a talent for that sort of thing.

In those days my tools were a number two pencil, a hard pink eraser and a sheet of white paper. I drew a bony man sprawled in the desert and an enormous sun radiating down on him. Dark ugly birds waited and watched. A second picture had an Egyptian soldier on top of a tank with a machine gun. He wore his black and white checked keffiyeh. Another picture showed bullets kicking sand and going up my father's leg, bits of cloth and flesh spraying out with the blood. Another had just a fist about the neck of a bird, almost a skeleton's hand. The bird's eyes were wide and lined with tiny veins. It had a startled expression and I remember laboring for an hour or more to get the look the way I had wanted it. Mother liked that one very much.

"That's a terrifying bird," she'd said. Look at those eyes, will you. And I *love* the veins. God the eyes give me the creeps. You got your talent from Grandpa Lester, my father. Are you aware of that? He wasn't an actual artist but he was in show business. Still, he was a creative type."

"You really like my pictures, Mama?"

"Well I'm not saying they couldn't use an extra line or two."

"So you don't like them?" I couldn't be sure with her.

This was 1984 and Mother was finishing her doctorate in clinical psychology at Temple University. After ten or so years away from school, she'd returned.

Her photos at that time had her looking very trim and pretty. She had big hair that went past her shoulders and the color of her hair changed every three or four months.

"Of course I like your pictures, Rhea, of course I do," she'd say. "I like them well enough. I'm just saying nobody's perfect. Remember, a person with a talent shouldn't flaunt it. That's all I'm saying. Average people hate a flaunter. It makes them uncomfortable. They start feeling they aren't as good as you, or as good as they ought to be. That's the way we are, everybody knows that."

Psychology probably wasn't the best choice for Mother.

I like to tell people I was a different sort of child illustrator. I was not an adult who drew pictures for children but a child who drew pictures for adults. Or maybe "adult" is too strong a word for my mother. And, yes, the years have gone by. I'm thirty-nine now and I have a ten year old son. Carlos, Jr. is a sweet and beautiful boy. Yet things haven't changed much, really. I still send Mother some of my illustrations, an occasional graphic novel. And she still wishes I'd do an extra line or two.

@wren&me1 Know how 2 open your soul? Wren says just do it. Not brave as her. 2 much darkness in Chicago. Maybe darkness goes with me.

TWO

I'M IN A CAB and the warmth of the morning is coming through the partially open window; the smell of exhausted fumes, too. Downtown Philly isn't much different from other big cities, they're all overcrowded and noisy and just breathing the air is the next best thing to suicide. I didn't want to leave Chicago but Philadelphia is my home and people have to go back home, occasionally. Also, let's be fair, my mother has given Carlos, Jr. and me the entire second floor of her brick row house in Elfreth's Alley. These are impressive homes with wood shutters and dormer windows. The rows face each other on a narrow cobblestone street. Elfreth's is located off Second between Arch and Race, part of Philadelphia's Old City and dates back to the 18th century. Mother likes to say my father won the house in a poker game years before I was born. Who knows. It's probably another one of her stories.

TODAY IS MY first session with Dr. Allison. Here's what I imagine telling her. I'll say, "After my husband left me and our son, I ran into the street and let a taxi hit me." I'm going to simply put it out there, no bullshit, no being charming, no getting-to-know you stuff. Then I will say, "When I was in the hospital – and later when I was home – I'd think more about my father than my husband. Not that I didn't think about Carlos, Sr., I did. And I *do* think about him. But with my father, it's different. I ache for my father. Is that unusual? Have you ever heard of such a thing? I feel this ache in the hollowness of my stomach, along the empty length of my arms. I am...I don't know...I'm *hungry* for him, this man I can't remember, this man who has suddenly made himself so known in his absence, his unavailability."

That's how I'm beginning it with Dr. Allison, for better or worse.

My mother tells me I'm one of millions who were raised without a father and that my divorce has given me a second chance to grieve losses from the present and the past, that my recent feelings about my father shows how strong a hold he has in my life.

I'm scared to death, of course. Therapy isn't what I've ever imagined for myself. Don't get me wrong, I like people and I have friends but I'm not a complainer and I don't chat well. Also I don't like listening to the problems of others – you know, my husband did this, my niece did that. Yada yada yada. I'm sorry, I just don't want to hear about it. Shoot me. Annoy somebody else. This especially includes the cell phone conversations of people I've never met. There's no escaping, either. Thanks to cell phones, I have to endure the complaints of strangers.

The other issue, *my* other issue, is Wren. I know I need to talk about her. But I'm not sure if there's a way to discuss Wren without presenting myself as a less than rational person. I know that Wren is a fiction, my invention, an invention I've know forever but one I have developed over the last ten or more years, at least ten. Let me also say right now, she doesn't *materialize* before me, I don't have conver*sations* with her, nor do we text or exchange emails, I want to be very clear about that. Premature conclusions and eye rolls will be considered smug and unwelcomed. I do not want to hear, "Okay, I have her number."

Nobody has anybody's number.

That said, there are nights I hear music. This is around 3:00, 3:30, deep into the

night or early morning. I'm not sure of the time, exactly. But whatever the time, it's too dark to see. I think I'm listening to a dinner music quartet. *The* Dinner Music Quartet, as

I've come to call them. There are two violins and a clarinet. And I know there's a piano; it's a grand piano. The quartet plays the same melody over and over, a Cole Porter tune – "Anything Goes." I want to believe this song was a favorite of my parents, or the sort of thing they liked. But I don't know for sure. I also realize I'm more than likely the only thirty-nine year old Cole Porter fan who is not in the theater.

This music is always in the distance. Say you lived in an apartment complex, the quartet would be playing in the apartment under you but maybe five or six doors down, it's that sort of distance. Many times I've turned to the dim green face of my clock radio, believing the music is coming from there. Wrong, wrong, wrong. It's in my head. And I experience this music not as a hallucination but as an oddly satisfying disturbance.

Why am I talking about this?

Because that's the way it is between Wren and me. I don't see her. I don't talk to her. But she is a remote and satisfying disturbance.

LIKE ME, WREN could also be a daughter my father would've avoided, not that I can definitively say this for either Wren or myself. Yet when I draw her, I will draw her with Daddy's ambivalence in mind. And I know every detail, I know the motion of her, the way she wears down the outer edges of her heels, how she likes to slouch low in a chair. I first sketch Wren's tiny

13

frame, skinny but moderately attractive. She's no more than five-three or four, and roughly a hundred pounds.

After the pencil comes the ink. The ink alone will push Wren into the world, will give her a presence, a force upon the landscape. She has the feet and the hands of a child, her small shoulders rounded, her face narrow with pointy cheekbones and a nose that's almost not there, a bit of a nose. That's followed by her piercings and her hair. Wren's polished metal rings cover the rims of both ears and two go through the left eyebrow. There's a small gold heart on a chain that is pierced through the left nipple. My publisher tells me the gold heart tests positive for males in the fifteen to twenty-one demographic. Her hair is another matter entirely. Nobody likes her hair except me. It's shaved smooth on the sides but the top is dark brown and ear-length and parted in the middle. Whether walking, running or turning her head, the hair is moving and reshaping itself.

Wren's in her mid-thirties now but has never fully quit her adolescence. She has a boring job in a dental lab but an exciting fantasy life. Her imagined villains are always underestimating her. Wren has cultivated a young vulnerable look, what she thinks of as her lure, the trap she'd use on her adversaries, if she had adversaries. Wren has attended Karate and Taekwondo classes since the age of twenty-two and she is very good at it but has never had to use any of it.

She's a Hero in Waiting.

Because "graphic" is in front of the word "novel" does not mean Wren is any less a literary invention than if she'd been born to a novel that had no illustrations. Wren isn't a cartoon or super hero or a cute little monster with teeth and *chutzpah*. I've planted her in *this* world; or I've tried my best to, anyway. She's in the world we all inhabit, limited to that world in the way we are all limited to it. Wren concerns herself with finding love and getting more interesting work. Her fantasy life gives her what she does not have in her actual life. In her fantasies she is attractive and daring and has the sort of adventures that are anything but safe.

That's the Wren I picture, the one I have always pictured. If you fault her reality, you must fault mine. And you must show me where the fault lies, where one thing does not follow the other. If you can do that, I'll not only accept the blame I will *join* your protest. I'll shout it with you, *This can't be right. What's happening here?*

A month ago a woman critic at the *Voice* reviewed my last graphic novel. She wrote, "...if you want to know Rhea Waye, you must get to know her 'alter ego' Wren." Of course I immediately emailed this critic and I told her there was nothing "alter" about it. Wren *is* me, what I think, what I feel, the actions and the thoughts of my life, my day to day. Except for the piercings and the odd hair, I even resemble her physically. Yet I may have been too quick on the trigger. Emails are dangerous things. Far too easy to write, far too easy to send. Wren does what I would like to do but *don't*. Well mostly I don't. So, yes, maybe a bit of an alter ego.

DR. ALLISON IS not a Freudian but she's not against Freud, either. I like the way she looks, thin and petite like Wren and me, a pale gray skirt and jacket, an ivory blouse, and a double string of tiny pearls. But her hair is gray. It's cut short to the ear, no strand out of place. The woman could very well be a French politician, a member of the *Assemblee Nationale*.

Dignified but persuadable.

Her office is the bottom floor of a Locust Street

Brownstone. Dark leather sofa and chairs and large Persian rugs decorate a room that has no windows. The lighting is indirect, a golden blush in an eternal twilight. And the scent of the room is the scent of her, a very muted cinnamon.

"Are you and my mother friends?" This is what I say immediately.

My mother is paying for my psychotherapy. Who does that? I'm an adult for God's sake. But Mother says, "my treat, Rhea, I insist." Like it's dinner and a movie.

"I know your mother, yes. We're colleagues."

You'd be astonished at the number of therapists who know each other in this town. Therapists in Philadelphia either know each other or know of you or at least have heard your name. Mother says they gossip, too. A lot. They're like debutants who talk about so-and-so's hideous fashion sense or how so-and-so had to give up his home in Bucks County or where-ever.

"But *are* you her friend?" I say. You can't get a clear answer from these people. What does "we're colleagues" mean? Do they discuss a paper, offer advice, have lunch, double date, what?

"Are you asking if I report back to her?"

"Yes, exactly. Report back."

"This is the problem when someone else pays for your therapy." Dr. Allison does not flinch, does not justify. "I understand you're a successful person. Novels, I've heard, graphic novels, something like that? At some point you might want to think about paying your own way."

"What has Mother told you?" I want to know.

"That your husband left you and you tried to kill yourself."

"She said *that*?"

Dr. Allison shrugs and writes something in the small brown leather notebook in her lap. "People try killing themselves everyday," the doctor says. "So, yes, she said that. She's concerned. And I told her I'd tell you our conversation – your mother's and mine – *if* you asked. I also told her it doesn't work the other way. I don't report back. But she knows that."

"...being a colleague."

"Being a colleague, you're right." Allison looks up and studies me for a moment then she looks down at her notebook and begins writing again. "This will be an issue for awhile. But you'll see, I don't betray my patients. I wouldn't last five minutes if I did that. Not that I expect you to believe me. People don't trust so easily."

Why is this woman writing? What have I said that's so interesting. I feel like I'm at a press conference.

"What else?" I say. "I want to know what else Mother told you."

"Your concerns with Wren. Is that the name, your character? It's a character in your writings, isn't it?"

"What about her." It's more a demand than a question.

"Your mother thinks you might be..." Dr. Allison hesitates, as if to find words that would both answer my question and calm me. "...too involved."

"It's what I do for a living, Doctor. Of course I'm involved." I take a breath and think to myself, *Relax. The woman isn't your enemy.* I smile to show I have everything under control but the smile is too fast and too nervous. "You're a very tactful person, I appreciate that. Thank you."

"Let me discuss this in a more straightforward way." Dr. Allison puts the cap on her black fountain pen, crosses her legs at the knee. Her legs are very slim and pretty. I wish I had legs like that. The Doctor says, "Your mother has heard you talking to Wren. You know, having conversations, that sort of thing."

"It's dialog. You read the dialog out loud to get a sense of its rhythm. God you'd think I was completely insane or something. I have been doing this for years – the dialog thing – but I've been doing it in Chicago and *not* in my mother's house. See that's the difference. I love my mother but she doesn't have a clue."

"So it's part of what you do, the writing?"

"I'm not crazy."

"Nobody's saying that."

My mother is a complex person whom I truly love but she's not the easiest person to live with. I guess it's better than staying in Chicago, though only a little better.

Dr. Elizabeth Waye.

God forbid anyone should forget the "doctor" part. She's a clinical psychologist who two years ago traded in a very successful Center City practice for a very successful syndicated radio program out of Philadelphia. 97.6 All Talk. *Five hundred and fifteen stations and counting, Rhea dear.* She now calls herself "Doctor Betty." She wants me to know that her life is more than simply being my mother. Which always makes me feel unbearably great.

"I don't believe it was the divorce that upset you. Leaving your husband, I mean. I believe it was painful but I don't believe it was that." Dr. Allison has placed her pen and her leather notebook on the small table next to her chair. "When we lose one person, we lose the others all over again." The doctor's voice is quiet and measured. "And each loss gives you a chance to mourn other losses."

"You and my mother."

"...pardon?"

"She's says this, too."

"Good. At least you're aware. If you lose a husband, you will have the chance to mourn a father. Or a mother. Or whoever left you, whether in death or by any other way. Leaving is leaving, isn't it? There's no rule saying who's first, who'll be mourned before the others. But the bigger the loss, the more likely the person will return. And these losses appear and reappear until you've done what you've needed to do."

I keep looking about her office; getting used to things, this situation. The walls are white and bare except for the diplomas and they are too far off to read. There are no pictures on these walls, no art work, no photographs. Nothing to show me her life.

"Do you still look for him?" Dr. Allison says.

"My Father? I go through periods."

"This is such a period?"

"...I don't know, I suppose, yeah."

"It's good you're here."

"We'll see."

TROUBLE IS COMING to Wren, let me be honest. Oh maybe it's only on the rim of her world looking in, but it's there. I've been far too eager to defend her. Four days ago I walked into my studio – early in the morning, five or five-thirty – and there on my drawing board were some pencil sketches I must have done the day before but I could not recall doing them. Yes, it's my work, that's clear, the drawings, the dialog, the style of it, everything. But I swear to you, I'd never approve of these changes.

Wren has quit her job. How does she pay her rent, how does she buy her food?

Now she sleeps during the day and goes out at night. I have six sketches of her having drinks at Megan's Bar on Walnut and nine sketches that show her bringing men back to her apartment. That's *not* what Wren does, not in her actual life and not in her fantasies. I'm sure there are test demographics that would approve of her new personality but this isn't her, that isn't how I see her.

Other pencil sketches have Wren traveling across rooftops, leaping from building to building. Another drawing has her silhouetted in front of a round moon, the night clear and filled with stars, her slim right leg extended, the leap frozen, graceful. One sketch is particularly disconcerting. Wren has landed on a rooftop, arms still above her head, and she's gripping a knife in her right hand. It's either a kitchen knife or a hunting knife, I'm not altogether sure, but the blade is very, very big. The sketch has moonlight glinting off the metal. Birds are also on the rooftops and the upper ledges. They're large and ugly with hunched shoulders and bony necks. Some are stretching their wings but most sit quietly.

I believe these birds are similar to the ones who watched my father. That's how I imagined them as a girl, anyway. They are perched everywhere – fifty or more, a few outlined by moon. The sketches of the birds are done with black ink and many of them have gold eyes.

Okay, I will say it.

This can't be right. What's happening here?

@wren&me1 Happening again. Wren says no worries. What follows u in Chicago follows u everywhere. Wish I had Wren's bravery, her fight.

THREE

MY GRANDFATHER HAS a semi-private room. A beige cloth curtain hides the bed area next to him. If you want to get me curious just hide behind a curtain. I'm not sure if the person on the other side is old or young. They do have younger patients here. But hints are minimal, the conversations too quiet to hear. Perhaps the patient can no longer speak, a stroke perhaps, throat cancer. What diseases steal a voice? Typically I just see the feet of the visitor and his lower legs. The gray gabardine with the loafers is visiting today -- that's what I call him – the gabardine visits on Monday afternoons. This gentleman has a cane and there is a rhythm to him. It's a rubber-tipped thump against the white and mint green tile. But the entrance to the room is on the other side of the privacy curtain. I've yet to get a good look.

"YOU DRAW ME too old," my grandfather says. I sent him two of my books last year, the two that featured him.
"Next time I'll do better."
"I look decrepit."
Our side of the room has two partially open windows with gauzy peach drapes. The walls are beige and there is an oil painting of men in red coats riding on the backs of horses. Dogs run with them, barking, howling. And the men and the horses and the dogs are

chasing a fox who's too far in the lead to look concerned. It's one of those dollar store paintings. The breeze is warm this afternoon and the curtains billow and twist.

My ninety-three year old grandfather's name is Lester. And he's a better guy now than he was thirty or more years ago and he was very terrific then. Old age seems to peel away everything but a person's essentials, it simplifies us. A young asshole will probably become an old unbearable asshole. A kind child will end up on a park bench, feeding the pigeons. It's fascinating how we can see the evil or the goodness of an elderly person, the shape and depth of the lines, the soft or hard way they look at you, the way life snaps beneath the skin. It's like they're preparing for judgment day, ridding themselves of the non-essentials.

"You got me in a wheelchair," Grandpa says. He's still on this old age thing and the pictures of himself in my novel. "I use a walker. Why can't you draw me using a walker? I can still stand up, you know. I can still walk."

"Okay. A walker, I promise."

"Write yourself a note. That's what I do."

"For you, Grandpa, anything."

"You're a good girl."

I bet he doesn't remember my name.

For the last nine years Grandpa Lester has been in an Alzheimer's facility on the 5200 block of Locust in Center City Philadelphia, the Little Sisters of Mercy. Nuns glide about the dimly lighted halls, some smiling and nodding at me, others ignoring me. The Little Sisters of Mercy are exactly that – *very* little. No nun is taller than four feet or so. When I walk among them, I feel like Dorothy in the *Wizard of Oz*. But there are no curly pointed shoes, no bright striped stockings. The sisters wear white hoods and black robes.

And nobody talks like a Munchkin. They also hire big people to do the heavy lifting but it's surprising how much the sisters can do themselves. This facility is a street or two from where Lester taunted the girls as a young man and hung with his friends at the corner drug store.

I THINK I hear the man with the cane going through the patient's closet, maybe the top drawer of a nightstand. It's so difficult to know. I wish the curtain didn't divide us. No, that's not true. I want the curtain there but I want x-ray vision to see through it. I want to catch the man with the cane. But who knows how much of this is fantasy? Like Mother says, "There's a dark side to your imagination, Rhea. Don't think there isn't." Doctor Betty could be right, after all, her listeners swear by her.

The patient on the other side of the curtain may have directed the gabardine man to fetch him something – whispered it or wrote it down on a piece of paper. Of course there's always the possibility that the patient can manage his own needs and was doing all that himself. This is what happens, my thinking has no off switch.

The other fantasy is even more creepy than the gabardine man searching the room of a helpless patient. I embarrass myself thinking about it. But I've always imagined J.D. Waye using a cane. Considering the injury, if my father kept his leg, he might need a cane for the remainder of his life. I'm *not* saying I believe it, okay? I'm saying it crosses my mind.

"GET OLD AND people avoid you."

"I'm not avoiding you, Grandpa." I'm sitting on the edge of his bed. Sunlight is bright and dusty in the room. "I've been living in Chicago, me and my family. But I'm in Philly now. Carlos, Jr. and I are staying with Mama. We can see each other more, you know, regularly and all. Okay? And you'd love Carlos, Jr. He's such a big boy. God I go nuts when people leave me."

"What do you know? How old are you, twelve?"

"Thirty-nine."

"Close enough."

It's a mysterious thing, Alzheimer's.

I'm always orienting Grandpa – that's what the staff calls it. Orienting. "Please help us orient the patient," they say. And you always orient "times three." That means I tell him the time, the person and where he is, and I do that over and over. The staff also pinned a name tag on me that reads Rhea Waye, Your Granddaughter in red Magic Marker. I am the "person" part of the "times three."

"What would Wren and I do without you?" I say to my grandfather. It's too true. When my grandfather appears with Wren in my books, he does so as the good guy who keeps her sane. Growing up, he did the same for me.

"You know women always want to talk about you," I tell him. "'God I wish I had that man in *my* life,' they'll say. Then I'll get, 'Did he actually make your grandmother disappear?' I get that all the time."

"It was a trick, making her disappear." His thinking has become very concrete over the years and he takes me too seriously. At the moment Grandpa is looking at the scrapbook I brought him, the newspaper clippings, the old photographs. "I was good at tricks," he says and strokes one of the clipping with his fingertips. "You ask anybody. I had the respect of the other performers. They always wanted to show me their act. 'Look at this, look at that,' they'd say. Excellent magicians, all of them. Or most of them. And they wanted my suggestions."

"I can imagine."

"Why would I lie?"

"Exactly. Not you, Grandpa."

"You're a sweet girl." He pats the top of my hand.

The scrapbook clippings and photos show Lester and Vera in their costumes. The photographs are done in black and white but Mother has talked about these photos and she can recall the color of their clothes. Lester wears his tux and bow tie and his cape with the red satin lining. He's tall and angular like me and has a moustache and slicked back hair. Vera is right beside him, the top of her head no higher than his chest. And what a lovely costume! It's a tu-tu with stockings, ballet slippers and a small tiara nested in her curls. She was as cute as she could be.

"You also used to saw Vera in half," I tell him.

"My goodness."

"Well not for real. She was your *very* glamorous assistant. Do you remember that?"

"She's a handsome woman." He is still examining Vera's photo. His forefinger touches Vera's face. It's a gentle touch as if he might wake her from the frozen state of her photograph.

Sometimes Lester has a clue; sometimes he doesn't.

Vera died fourteen years ago. Mother has her features, her dark hair, her big dark eyes. I didn't get any of that. Mother says I look like my father's older sister, a woman with artistic abilities but not much else. Grandma Vera was what people call "willowy" and her photographs show her as a sepia-tinted knockout.

"I have a little boy, Grandpa. His name is Carlos."

"What is he? Like a Dominican?"

"Puerto Rican."

"Dominicans have pretty skin."

I SEE THE cane with the rubber tip between the man's feet. I know he must be sitting because twice his brown loafers left the floor simultaneously and hovered there. I also know the man is talking to the patient but the talk is too quiet for me to hear. The privacy curtain and Lester reminiscing about the clippings and the photos don't help the situation, either.

I imagine Wren standing next to the thick beige curtain by an empty wood chair. Metal rings are hooked about her right ear and along her eyebrow and the rings catch the fluorescent light. She is always in black and her clothes don't change with the seasons. I have thought about another jacket or what-have-you in the summer months but decided against it. Superman doesn't have a summer suit, why should Wren? I actually do think about these thing. The Wren brand, so-to-speak. There is a leather jacket with zippered pockets, tight jeans on skinny legs, black hightop sneakers with gray white tips.

So for better or worst, that's my girl's costume.

Wren first squats down and looks under the curtain. And she looks under it the way an automobile mechanic might first look under a car. No laying on his back, no sliding himself beneath it. Just a peek. Do we have a fluid leak, a hole in the muffler?

Let me check off the easy things, the mechanic thinks. That's what I believe Wren is doing. She's checking the easy stuff. Are there two people behind the curtain? Are we talking men or women or both? How old is the man with the cane? My father was twenty-four during the Yom Kippur War. He'd be in his early sixties now. Wren would be the sort who'd search for J.D. Waye, she has that personality. Track him down, leave no stone unturned, a Canadian Mounty in Goth clothing, that's our Wren.

LESTER IS TALKING about getting older.

"I don't feel *any* different than I did when I was twenty," he says. "Maybe in the morning. I'll be honest, the mornings are pretty damn awful. Mornings are rough. But catch me at ten-thirty, eleven, and I'm a twenty year old inside this piece of shit body. See that's the trouble with people, nobody takes the time to know the *per*son. It's body, body, nothing but that. I watch the TV, I see the commercials. I'm not an imbecile. You got me at death's door."

"Please don't say that."

"Can't you draw me with a little hair, a couple of teeth?"

"I don't want to think about you not being here."

"I bet you got the coffin picked out."

"That's *not* true, Grandpa."

Mother bought her father's coffin two weeks ago from Wholesale Caskets Online. It's an 18 gauge steel with a light purple finish and a white velvet interior that includes a pillow. Originally it was $5,995.00 but mother says she got it for $898.00. A person can get anything on the Internet.

"Hey wait 'til you get old," Grandpa Lester says. "You think this is fun, loose skin and a prostate the size of a baseball? This shits."

I've tried empathizing with Lester; even pictured myself as a grandmother. Some old arthritic thing. This usually happens at two-thirty or three in the morning. None of it has a good finish. I've got all the bad facial lines, my eyes are too recessed, shoulders are humped and stiff from too much time at the drawing board. I become the W. W. W., the Wicked Witch of the West. I'm dressed in black thready robes and square-tipped shoes and I battle Dorothy and her three friends – Bert, Ray and Jack – and send them back to Kansas which, in my dreams at least, always seems a worse fate than

Oz.

I'm the rickety W.W.W. your parents warn you about, the one they post on the refrigerator door, the one beside your talented pre-school child's picture of a stick figure family in front of a house with a curl of chimney smoke and a big yellow sun. This child has also named each of these figures. There is Daddy and Mommy and a stick figured hamster named Bob.

"Beware of this evil woman," the sign says. "Do not accept candy or beverages from this person. Report her to your teachers, to your local pastor or rabbi, anyone who has a kinder face and more colorful clothes." In these early morning thoughts my own family treats me no better than strangers. My would-be grandchildren flee their homes and scream, "Granny is coming! Granny is coming! God help us! Hurry, hurry! Get in the car, everybody!"

I AM STILL listening to Grandpa Lester but I'm also looking over his shoulder at Wren. She is standing next to the beige privacy curtain, head gone from view. Her hand motions to me to go to her. Sunlight is laying across the white and mint green tile floor and there's a brilliant divide between us.

"Stop that," I whisper to her.

"Stop what?" Lester wants to know.

"Nothing, Grandpa. Me being silly."

"You're getting too old for that."

Wren has withdrawn her head from behind the curtain. She grins at me, or I think I see her grinning. Next she points to Lester with a forefinger. Then Wren uses the same finger to rotate tiny invisibles circles near the side of her head, the international You Are Crazy sign.

I can't quit smiling at her.

"What so funny?" Lester says.

"I'm just happy to be here." And I am, truly.

"Nobody's happy here."

"Are you kidding?" I say. "You saved my life. When I was a little girl, I loved being with you. Those tricks, the way you made me smile, I remember it all. It's the only memory I trust, believe me."

My smile leaves me when I turn back to glimpse at Wren and she's not there. A momentary hot-cold shiver goes through my chest. Hey this is *my* image of her, and I haven't dismissed anybody. That's when I look at the rim of the curtain and I see Wren's skinny legs and her black hightops with the gray-white tips. The man with the cane has gone. I hear talking, though, a distant cadence. But I can't understand the words.

FOUR

"I DON'T LIKE this place," Carlos, Jr. is saying. "You promised kids. Where are the kids?" My ten year old has been pissy since we arrived. He's standing beside me now in the new studio. Mother had it built to lure us back to Philly. White walls, polished blond wood floors, the sunlight is everywhere. "I mean who do I play with, exactly?"

Carlos is a Chicago boy and Philadelphia simply doesn't interest him.

"You've never been to Philly," I say. "How d'you know whether you'll like it or not? Give things a chance, baby. Okay?"

"We've been here a *month*."

"Well oh God, let's pack our bags."

My son has black hair and dark brown eyes like Carlos, Sr. but he is skinny and small like his mom, small for a ten year old, anyway. And the boy truly frets about me. I know he does and I've no idea how to stop him from doing it. I haven't been projecting enough strength of character recently.

"Does Philadelphia make you feel better?" My son wants to know.

"I felt fine in Chicago."

"No you didn't. You cried a lot and walked in front of a cab. You absolutely *didn't* feel fine. People who feel fine do ordinary things. They cook dinner, watch TV. Don't tell me you were fine."

Where is that infallible mother when you need her?

I try to touch his cheek with the palm of my hand but he backs away. It's going to take awhile for him to forgive me.

I ignore his pouty attitude and say, "So you think I wasn't doing that well? Okay, there's truth to that – *prob*ably. Mr. Wiseguy. Since when did you become this amazing rocket scientist?"

"A retard could get that. Matt brought you home in a wheelchair. A *wheel*chair, for god-sake. Mothers don't do what you did, they don't run in front of cabs. They have, you know, responsibilities. Obligations. People depend on them."

"Anyone I know?"

"I hope you aren't being funny."

"Didn't I apologize? How many times am I supposed to apologize, Carlos?" I know I should have patience but I get weary, occasionally.

"Just don't turn this into a joke."

"You tell me a number and I'll do it, okay? I'll do my apologies again. Thirty, a hundred, what? I love you more than my own life. I know Mommy did a crazy dumb thing. I know it, believe me, I know. Nobody can beat me up more than I beat myself up. I made a mistake, it's terrible. What more can I tell you? What more can I do?"

"You don't feel sorry. You feel guilty."

"Oh boy. Great." Carlos, Jr. and Doctor Betty have been talking. "That totally sounds like your grandmother."

"Feeling sorry is about the *other* person. Feeling guilty is about *your*self."

Thank you, Doctor Betty.

"It could be both, baby. Why not both?" I'm trying to stay calm; I'm trying to be a good mom, maybe give my darling child a teachable moment. "Have you thought about that? Not one thing or the other but both? People hardly ever feel just one thing. Maybe a mother can feel sorry about her boy and feel guilty that she did a really stupid thing."

"But a *wheel*chair." The kid won't let go of it. I obviously scared him to death. He says, "You had a couple of black eyes and bandages up to your neck. I mean I was feeling like an orphan, or practically an orphan. And Matt's telling me to take it easy. Like this is some everyday thing. You know, like tomorrow things would be different and crap."

"Watch the language."

"I said crap."

Matt and his partner Clyde were our neighbors, the apartment next to us. They were lovely people, very good neighbors. And they adored Carlos, Jr. – believe it or not, almost everybody does – and they put up with Carlos, Sr.

I'll give my husband credit, though, he was always polite to Matt and Clyde and never embarrassed them with stupid comments. No cute macho gay jokes, no prancing around, no lisping sentences with a hand on hip, no anxious talk about turning our son gay, he did good. Also, Carlos, Sr. and Matt are both chefs. So they had the restaurant business in common. I think they enjoyed complaining to one another. The restaurant life isn't the sort of business you'd wish on your worst enemy. But the people in it love it, particularly the chefs.

MORE SKETCHES I don't remember doing. I'm not saying I didn't do them, I'm just saying I've no recollection of doing them. It's 2:15 in the morning and I can't sleep; I can't even get comfortable enough to rest. My pillow is too hot, my shoulders ache – the right one, especially – and my mind has become chatty without purpose. So I have wandered into my studio. Moonlight is coming through the skylight and the windows and it's a silver color on the walls and the polished wood floor.

When did I do these pictures?

I'm at my drawing board and looking at the pencil sketches, admiring each piece begrudgingly as if the work belonged to a rival artist. And who knows, perhaps I'm not altogether wrong on that. Aren't we our own worst enemies? Don't we kick ourselves more than others kick us? Okay, some don't do that but, let's face it, most of us do. The new sketches are more austere than the first batch, harsher lines, bolder, also more intimidating and violent.

One sketch has Wren on the other side of the privacy curtain in Grandpa Lester's room. She is behind the man with the cane. Shadows hide most of her. Across from the man and Wren is a hospital bed. Someone is in the bed but I can't see the person's face and I don't know who it would be, I don't even know if it's a man or a woman.

What fascinates is the part of Wren's face that is free from the shadows. She's smiling, I think, an upturn at the edges of her mouth.

"What are you doing?" I whisper to her.

"...you know."

The voice is coming from the far left corner of the studio, or maybe I imagine it. Moonlight has left the corners of the room dark. My back straightens and I look up from the sketches. My stomach begins cramping. I try to relax by slowly releasing a deep breath.

"Carlos? Hello?" I don't think it's my son but I say his name, anyway.

A small slim figure darts from the left corner to the right. It's not much more than a quick but dim light. I hear a car passing below my studio and I want to believe it's only the headlights of the car.

"...hello?" I can barely hear my own word.

There is no answer and I'm thinking maybe I need to get a grip. I haven't been sleeping well. My thoughts keep me awake. These thoughts are nothing in particular, nothing dramatic. What will I have for dinner? What should I wear tomorrow? I have two white silk blouses that need a dry cleaner. But the dry cleaner is too expensive. I ought to just buy a new blouse. This is how my mind goes. I'll worry that I don't read enough. When was the last time I bought a book? My last book was an audiobook. Isn't that cheating? I worry about my weight. My diet sucks. A fat single woman with a child doesn't have a chance in this world. I know I'm thin but I could *become* fat. It would take less than a week. A pizza here, a gallon of rum raisin Haagen Dazs there. I worry about my drinking. I should cut my three glasses of chardonnay down to two. Two is healthy. Three is alcoholic. I worry about the music. I occasionally hear the Cole Porter song "Anything Goes" by the Dinner Music Quartet – that's what I call them – and I hum along but inside my head. I don't know where the music comes from, a nearby radio, the CD player nextdoor, I don't know. What's worse, I used to listen to the same song by the same quartet at night in Chicago. And now it's followed me to Philadelphia. Sleep is a gift I seldom get.

When did I do these pictures?

I look at another sketch, this one inked over the pencil lines. I'd planned to give it just a glance but it snags me and holds on. Wren has a knife to the man's throat, the man with the cane. Her face is next to his face, cheek to cheek, and she's grinning. It's what Carlos, Sr. used to call a "fat shit-eating grin." Shadows are covering the man's face but not his neck and the big

35

knife at his neck. I think of a caption but it makes no sense. *Do you love me now?* A knife to the throat is no way to get what you want, especially love. That's my first thought. Or no way to *believe* you got it honestly. And Wren's grin has a gloating feeling to it. I picture a thought bubble over her head. It says, "Wouldn't you like to be me, Rhea? Would you like to be here with a knife at his throat."

Do you love me now?

"ARE YOU BETTER? Can you tell me that?" Carlos, Jr. is leaning his elbows on my white drawing table, the morning sunlight bright behind him. It gives a luminous edge to his dark hair. "I mean you don't feel like you're going to run out and hop in front of any cabs, or whatever?"

"That's a one time deal."

"Because you're it, you know. If you go, it's me and Grandma."

"Don't give me that. You like her plenty."

"She keeps giving me stuff."

"What a problem." Sometimes Carlos, Jr. slays me. "I don't see you saying no. I don't see you saying, 'Please, Grandma, don't give me these jeans and socks and all this underwear. What *I* see is a lot of kisses on the cheek and you telling her, 'Oh Grandma, you're so crazy great.' Isn't that what you say? How she's so crazy great?"

"It's a saying."

"I know what it is, Mr. Smooth."

"You know she has a gun," my boy says. Whispers it, really.

"What do you mean 'gun.' You mean like a pistol, a firearm?" Right away I feel my anxiety level rise. Why would Mother even go there? "Did grandma actually tell you that? That she has a gun in the house?"

"In her nightstand," Carlos, Jr. says. He can see I'm upset and he tries to calm me. "She *told* me it was dangerous, Mom. She just didn't want it to be a surprise. She said women living alone in a big city ought to have a gun."

"You leave that gun alone, it's no toy. Promise me."

"I'm not a moron."

"*Promise* me," I say again. "This isn't a video game."

"Okay. God. I promise."

I think Dr. Betty is thrilled that Carlos, Jr. is here. Maybe talking to him about the gun isn't so bizarre. Better he know about it and know it's dangerous. They've become very tight buds, at least from Mother's perspective. And, yes, she does to my son what she did to me. The woman buys him stuff; that's her M.O., so-to-speak. She has done that with me forever. I had enough Barbie dolls to start my own roller derby franchise. Besides the jeans and the socks and whatnot, my son now has himself a gaming machine and a 52 inch flat screen TV. He's battling Orcs and dragons with magic spells. Heavy duty frost. Fireballs. Chain lightning. It's seriously scary. And that's *so* Mother. Her mantra is, I love you. Have a flat screen TV.

We give our love the way we can give it.

"I've made a lovely little studio for you," Mother had said in her last email. This is before we left for Philly. "It's a cheerful room with lots of sunlight. You can do your drawings or your novels, whatever it is you do."

Nobody would get a hint from that email but I've sent her all seven of my graphic novels. I realize it's not what people think of when they think "literature" but all of these novels have had respectable sales, and all were personally autographed. *To my darling Mother*. But does she acknowledge any of it, does she care enough to give credit where credit is due? No, no, never. And while we're on this subject, here is another example of her – I don't know what to call it – her cocoon*ness*: "I'm thrilled that you and the boy are coming to Philadelphia," Mother's email said. "It will give me a fine chance to get to know our young man." This might seem nice enough but I would like you to notice how she doesn't use the word "grandchild" or the phrase "*my* grandchild." My. As in *her* grandchild. Okay, it's a little thing. And I'm paranoid, I'm a bitch, I get it. But then her email ends cryptically with, "You know, Miss Rhea Waye, we have creative people here in Philadelphia, too."

WTF? Seriously.

I DON'T KNOW if Wren slits the throat of the man with the cane. I can't find any sketches that show her actually doing the act. Maybe they're simply posing for me. That's what it starts feeling like, except I shaded the man's face and have no idea of his expression. And I'm still guessing this is my work. It *looks* like mine. God it's is all so bizarre. No sense making it easy for myself. But there Wren is, cheek to cheek with the man's shadowed face, smiling for the camera, the knife as long as her forearm.

All five new sketches are about the man, either direct or inferred. Wren is either disappearing behind the privacy curtain or she's sneaking up on him or coming out of the darkness toward the back of him, that sort of thing.

CARLOS, JR. IS now sitting next to me as I do my work. He's always loved to

watch his Mom draw. And it's comforting to have him here. Mostly my son will smile and nod and occasionally he'll say, "Wow," or "Oh Mom." It's like having my personal Greek chorus.

But this morning Carlos, Jr. is very squirmy. My soon to be ex-husband used to call it Jonesin'. You scratch, you can't keep still, it's like waiting for your dealer. When my child gets in that state I know he wants to talk but he's not sure if he'll upset me.

"You really need to gets some friends," I say. And this is true. My son is a very social person and Carlos without friends isn't the calmest person on the planet. "I'm surprised you're not outside recruiting."

"I gave our phone number to that guy."

"What guy? What're you saying?"

"The guy in the room with Grandpa."

"Behind the curtain? *That* guy?"

"He's a kid, Mom. He's like two years older than me."

"You talked to him?"

"He was asleep. You should see him. His face and his arms are all bandaged. I read his chart. There's something wrong with his pigments. What's a pigment?"

"Nevermind that. I just can't believe you. That's personal information," I say. I can't believe it. Where was I? "Carlos, you can't go reading a person's *chart*. You're a smart kid, you know better than that."

"I left the phone number under his pillow."

I'd brought Carlos, Jr. with me to see Grandpa Lester. I thought getting my son

out of the house and away from TV and video games would be good. Of course he was

bored out of his mind. Except for the nuns, he really loved the nuns. I think he liked being taller than them. He kept wanting to know if he could help out, carry something, lift something. Carlos can be a trip.

"Stop that tapping," I say. My darling boy's hitting his foot against the rungs of his wood stool and it's driving me nuts. He does annoying things like that all the time. I adore him but I wonder if little girls hit their feet on the rungs of stools. Intuitively, I think six of one half a dozen of the other. My son hits his foot against the stool again. "Hey, Carlos, did you hear me?"

"I'm not doing anything."

"You're tapping your foot."

"Yeah. So?"

"Would you like to say something to Mommy?"

"You mean talk?"

"Uh-huh. Let's start there."

"You're not going to like it."

"...oh I bet."

I'M CALMER NOW, basically. God you should have seen me in Chicago. I *was* a hyperventilator in Chicago, the last days weren't my best. See I think Philadelphia has a good effect on me, Independence Hall, the Liberty Bell, cheese steaks. I'm a steadier individual here, more solid. Chicago had too many haunts, things Carlos, Sr. and I used to do together. There isn't a street in that city that didn't remind me of a life I didn't have anymore. You love a person and you trust that person and you think your marriage is peachy fine. But then you find out it's your side that's peachy fine. The other person's side is only fine if they can live with somebody named Ivy Landis. I couldn't believe it. Ivy *Landis*? Who the fuck, excuse me, is Ivy *Landis*?

I met Carlos, Sr. in Germantown high school in Philly. *High* school, okay? We started dating in ninth grade, that's almost twenty-five years ago – both of us fifteen, I think, Carlos three months older than me but never wiser.

That's twenty-five years of my mother asking the walls and the furniture, "Why a Puerto Rican?" This was a question she always asked of things and not people.

From day one Carlos and I got along. We were like your typical Ying and Yang. Your Batman and Robin, your Green Hornet and Kato. I'm serious as anything, we were this really sloppy love song. The Carpenters or somebody. Or Bobby Vinton and "Blue Velvet." We protected each other or like people say in Philly, we had each other's backs. That's one of many terrific things about being married to a Puerto Rican. Or at least *my* Puerto Rican. If some guy put the moves on me or gave me grief, Carlos would let him know how much God and the angels disapproved. Maybe other nationalities could do the job but I don't believe they'd do it as well.

Ivy Landis.

You think you know somebody. I'm talking about Carlos, Sr. here. I've never met Little Ms. Home Wrecker. But I imagine her as a former cheerleader with blond hair and hard perky tits. That was years and years ago, I mean *years* ago. Now the woman is an early forties realtor who's prematurely gray and has fat rolls and likes cruises to the Greek Islands and cosmetic surgery. Not that I've ever met her, you understand. It's just a vengeful fantasy.

What pulled the life out of me was Carlos, Sr. I shouldn't expect people to love me the way I want to be loved, that's what Mother says. It feels pushy and unrealistic, you know? But I don't get how a person can do that, be kind and loving and leave you.

I never saw it coming.

"WHERE DID YOU find this?" I say.

"In my bed."

We're still in the studio and my son and I are seated on wood stools in front of the drawing board. The morning sun brings too much light and the brightness reflects off the floor and the white walls. I need to buy shades for the windows before I go blind.

"So you woke up and there it was?" I say. "Is that what you're telling me? You sure you didn't come into Mommy's studio and find it on her drawing board with the others?"

Carlos, Jr. has just pulled a folded piece of drawing paper from the back pocket of his jeans and handed it to me. It's a sketch like the others but not quite like the others. It's not about the man with the cane.

"Why would I do that?"

"I'm just asking."

"But why wouldn't you trust me?"

It has nothing to do with trusting or not trusting but I don't say that to my son. I don't say anything. I get weary having to explain and defend myself. It's my belief that I've drawn all of the sketches, including the one I'm now holding. But I don't recall working on them and I don't understand my motive for drawing them. Every artist has a style, though, and I know my style when I see it.

It's another sketch of Wren on the roof of a building. The night is clear and starry and with only a sliver of moon. There are four large dark birds behind her and they have gold eyes. I don't know who has a fondness for whom. Do I invite these birds or do they invite themselves? Wren is squatting at the roof's edge, skinny arms on her knees. She's gripping the handle of a knife and the blade's tip rests on the concrete edge of the roof between her black hightops. Carlos, Jr. is next to Wren, he's also squatting, one arm leaning on her slender shoulder. I feel the hard beat of my heart at my neck and I have to force myself to take a breath. It scares me to see him with her. It scares me more not to recall what I've done.

Wren and my son are waiting for someone, keeping watch on the sidewalk below. I believe they're expecting the man with the cane. Isn't it all about him?

I think it is, I think so. And I imagine that they see the man and leap from the rooftop like a pair of elegant superheroes. They land in front of him and Wren stabs at his neck and chest far too many times. My son helps by holding the man's legs and preventing his escape. I know that, too.

@wren&me1 What am I supposed 2 c that I don't c? Chicago kept 2 many secrets from me. Maybe Philly okay. Love & kisses from Wren & me!

FIVE

"NO RECOLLECTION?"

"The sketches are mine, I know that. I'm not a complete mental case." No, I'm not but I'm certainly beginning to sound like one. Could I get more defensive? Then I say, "I mean a person can tell their own drawings. I just don't remember working on them. Okay? That's what I'm trying to say."

Dr. Allison is wearing another pale gray outfit, this time pleated pants instead of a skirt. She also has matching gray leather flatties. Very color coordinated. I begin wondering about the amount of planning that goes into what looks good with what.

"Tell me your thoughts."

"Your clothes are lovely."

"...that's what your thinking? Clothes?" Dr. Allison looks up from her notebook

and smiles. She puts the cap on her fountain pen. "I'm glad you find my clothes lovely but we should think about your compliment, the context of it."

"But I *like* your clothes." I do; it isn't an insult.

"All of that's fine." Her legs are crossed and she starts to flip her flattie up and down on her heel. It's silent but noticeable, as if her shoe has become impatient. "Let me talk about therapists and what we do. We try to help by listening to our patients and talking to them about the words they say to us. And not only your words, it is also *when* you say your words. It's when you *choose* to give me this compliment. So here we are, you and I, we're talking about the drawings you don't remember doing, drawings that hint of violence. Drawings that involve knives. Involve your son. And when you and I begin talking about this, where do your thoughts go?"

"...clothes."

"The furthest thing from violence."

I shouldn't have said anything about the sketch Carlos, Jr. showed me. Saying a thing out loud has a way of turning it real. Wren and my son are squatting at the edge of the roof along with the big dark birds. I am sure these are the same birds who waited for my father to die. It's too creepy, the hunched black wings, the gold eyes. They are scavengers waiting for a meal.

"It was supposed to be a compliment," I say.

"Yes, I know. And I thank you."

"I didn't mean to insult you."

"I don't feel insulted. Your compliment is very generous and I'm pleased that you like my clothes. But what we say can serve many purposes. That's how our minds work. That's why I want you to think about the context. About why you chose to give me a compliment at that particular moment."

Her office is air-conditioned but I can't hear the air conditioner or see the vents. There are no windows and the lighting is so subtle I can't see its origin. Both the lighting and the cool air are perfect and mysterious. The office has a warmth to it, the dark wood and the dark leather, the oriental throw rugs. And it has a vague cinnamon fragrance. This sort of room makes me want to go backstage and see how it works.

"Okay but I know the sketches are mine," I say. "And If I *know* that – know they're mine – then I don't get your point, really."

"...uh-huh. I can see that." Dr. Allison starts writing

in her notebook. She's talking to me as she's writes. "I know how to spell Mississippi. And I could spell it for you right now but I can take it or leave it. I've no feelings one way or the other about spelling Mississippi. In this case my lack of feeling is understandable, yes? Spelling Mississippi is *always* boring." Now she looks at me, her pen hovering an inch or two above the leather notebook. "You also forget your feelings. But here's the difference between you and I. You listening?"

"...yes. Of course." What else would I be doing?

"You forget your feelings not because they're too boring to mention but because these feelings are too dangerous to know."

I say nothing; I'm not sure how to answer.

"...dangerous enough to hide," she says. Just in case I missed it.

Her words go into me like sharp hot wires. Don't get me wrong. The tone of the words are calm and good tempered. But tears swell along the rims of my eyes and trail the line of my cheeks and I do not know why. All I know is that Dr. Allison can see something in me that I can't see in myself. Or maybe not, maybe the woman doesn't have a clue but thinks she does.

Right. Who am I kidding?

A WEEK BEFORE Carlos, Jr. and I left for Philadelphia, my mother had called me at eleven-thirty, maybe closer to midnight. Worst timing ever, believe me. This was the night my soon-to-be ex-husband decided to come over and get the remainder of his things from the hall closet. These things include a tennis racket he never used and a tan leather jacket he hated. Did I mention he'd been drinking? "...just chardonnay," he says. Like that doesn't count. So this visit obviously had more to do with telling me what was on his mind than gathering his shit.

God it was a terrible fight. How can you despise a person and keep it a secret for years and years? No one hit anyone but once the yelling started it didn't quit until Carlos, Sr. had shut the door behind him. Slammed it, if you want the truth. Did it hard enough to knock a silver framed wedding photograph off our mahogany end table. Again I've no details, or not every detail. Chunks of that night are missing. It's more a sense of what happened, the way we cling to the feelings in a dream but don't recall most of the images.

I may have a tumor.

Such a possibility has occurred to me. Don't tumors do that, make pieces of your life unavailable? I imagine myself in a recovery room with a bandaged head and flowers on my nightstand. White and pink carnations, not roses. Carnations say, *Don't worry. Things get better*. Roses are very different. Roses are what you put atop a casket before cranking it into the hole and throwing on the dirt.

Never give roses to a person with a brain tumor.

Twenty-five minutes after Carlos, Sr. left the apartment, I got the phone call from Mother. She was hesitant and soft-spoken, not her usual self. I felt uncomfortable right off.

"...dear? Hello? Did I wake you?"

"I'll call you back."

"How ... are you feeling?"

"Tomorrow, Mother."

"We haven't talked in *two* weeks." There's a poutiness to her tone. I know that poutiness. All her inflections have messages and this one is a big favorite: *I raised you without a husband, how about you give me a minute of your valuable time.* "What have you heard from Carlos?" she wants to know.

"Nothing. Since when are you worried about

Carlos?" That's an honest to God

Fact. Carlos, Sr. doesn't enter her mind. Ever. Usually she refers to him as "that Puerto Rican."

Oh. Wait. I may have a tumor but I'm not stupid. Now I get the reason for Dr. Betty's call. "He just talked to you, didn't he? Don't lie to me Mother. I can hear it in your voice. Carlos talked to you."

"We're worried about our Rhea."

"*We*? Excuse me, what's the '*we*' thing?"

"YOU'VE LOST YOUR history," Dr. Allison says. She has stopped writing her notes to look at me. "When we lose our past, it becomes impossible to make sense of the present – why we do what we do. We'll get angry at some trivial thing, and we *know* it's trivial, we know our behavior is crazy or disconnected, but we'll get angry anyway. It's only when we look at our history that we see why we felt these disconnected feelings, why we acted the way we did. This is the purpose of therapy, to put the past back in the past where it belongs."

"You people obsess about the past," I tell her.

"But aren't you also doing that? You're acting out behaviors from a history you can't remember. And you act out these feelings everyday. Or you give them to Wren and have her act them out. Isn't that obsessing, too?"

I look about Dr. Allison's office. I have been looking about her office the entire session, practically. She and I are face-to-face in dueling leather chairs and my choices are limited. I can either look at her or the office. Right now I prefer the office, its throw rugs, its mahogany desk and high ceiling.

"What's the saying?" I'm asking myself more than her. It's quiet for a moment or two. I recall the saying and I answer my question out loud, " Oh I know. 'Let sleeping dogs lie,' isn't that it?"

"But here's your dilemma." She is writing again. Each time she writes I feel as if I have failed in an unfathomable way, that my shortcomings are being listed. She says, "If you can't remember your past, if it's too painful for you – and that's what it is, you know, too painful – then how do you decide which dog needs to run and which dog needs to lie?"

You can't argue with her and win.

"It's just a saying." I whisper this.

"You have actions with no context."

"You like that word."

"Context? Yes, very much." Dr. Allison smiles, it's the first big one. Her teeth are small and even and with lots of pink gum. "You do these actions, the drawings of Wren, the ideas the drawings represent. But you think of them as a puzzle. They confuse you. The drawings *you* do, the statements *you* make with those drawings, you see these things as scary. In my business, the therapy business, rogues feelings are the most dangerous. That sort of 'feeling' has no home."

"No context."

"Yes, exactly." Dr. Allison's words are calm and steady, her mood is no different than her office, all cool air and indirect lighting. I half expect to hear elevator music in the background, violins playing "Eleanor Rigby," the woman who kept her face in a jar. "Why do you think that is?" the doctor is saying. "Why are you pushing your past out of sight? Why do you feel your past but cannot give that feeling to the right sleepy dog and tell it to go lie down?"

"PSYCHOTHERAPY SAVED MY life," my mother says. This is the day after Carlos, Jr. and I arrived in Philadelphia, before my first appointment with Dr. Allison. Mother and I are sitting in the living room. Carlos is upstairs in his new bedroom doing God-knows-what. "When Daddy left, I was crazy just like you," Mother says. "Well maybe not exactly like you. I didn't throw myself in front of a taxi. But you know what I mean. Men. What are we supposed to do? Too bad we can't become lesbians."

"I don't need psychotherapy."

"Everybody needs psychotherapy. It'll be my treat, Rhea. Just show up."

"You don't treat people to that."

"There's nothing wrong with support, particularly after a divorce. Be thankful I care enough to help."

"But it's *therapy*, Mother. It's not a gift certificate to a spa or whatever. Isn't therapy a personal thing, a personal decision? I mean it's your life. *My* life. I'm sure people don't do that. I think there's a rule somewhere."

"Why worry yourself about the finances?"

"I have money."

"I'm treating my daughter, you act like it's a crime." This was one of those late morning conversations, each of us with a cup of coffee, Mother still in her pale green kimono with pink cherry petals on it. God knows how old that kimono is, I remember it when I was a kid. "You're not the only person with money," she tells me. "Let me do a little gesture, something. Learn how to rely on others, Rhea. I'm not saying you should do that all the time, relying on others. I know how self-sufficient you are, and I'm all for being self-sufficient. But so many things happened in Chicago. It would be nice to talk to a person, someone you could trust."

"All what things?"

"...pardon?"

"You said, 'so many things happened in Chicago.' And so I'm saying, 'All what things?' What were the other things? I don't remember *other* things. I remember Carlos talking about this Ivy Landis and how if I loved him I'd understand. Like we were going steady and he wanted to take Ivy fucking Landis to the prom. Excuse the language, what sort of love is he talking about – I should under*stand* him? Oh I understand him all right.

But I don't get what you mean, 'so many things happened in Chicago.' You mean me

walking in front of a taxi? Or *other* things besides the taxi. Because if you're talking about stuff besides the taxi, then I don't know. Then I'm lost."

"Your husband called me, Rhea. You didn't know Carlos called? He said you cut up the furniture with a knife. A kitchen knife, he said."

"Carlos said that?"

"The furniture cushions, mainly."

"And you believe him?"

"I don't know what to believe." Mother had another sip of her coffee. Her free hand clutching the top of her kimono. "He was scared to death, that boy. You should've heard. I've never thought he could get so anxious. You must've scared the poop out of him."

"Oh c'mon, Mother. Please."

"Let me call Dr. Allison."

"Who's that? Some friend who needs patients?"

"You're lucky you have me, Rhea. There are good therapists and bad ones. But I a know this city and I know the therapists in this city. Dr. Allison specializes in divorce and grief – people who suffer lose."

"I'm sure she's a nice person."

"I don't know what sort of person she is. That's her business. But I *do* know she a good therapist."

"Why are you so ready to believe Carlos?" I say. "Why is your own daughter automatically the guilty party? Have you ever thought about that, your bias? Have you thought about it once? No, you haven't, I know you. You'd rather believe a man who you've never liked a day in your life than your own daughter."

"The man's a Puerto Rican."

"That's you reason?"

"I know Carlos. He'd rather jump off a bridge than sound anxious. Latin men are

like that, they're proud men. And he was scared."

SIX

I WAKE AND my undershirt and cotton boxers are soaked with sweat; the sheets and pillow case, too. My hands and my shoulders won't quit shaking. The therapy must be doing things to me, I know it. That's what I get for listening to Mother. My bedroom is dark except for a rectangle cut of moonlight coming through the half-open window and across the pine floor. I had a dream, what the hell was that dream? The digital clock on the nightstand reads 2:36 AM. I still hear the downtown traffic a couple of blocks away. But the "city that never sleeps" idea is bogus. The city does sleep but it does it in shifts. That means someone is always awake to irritate the ones who are trying to sleep. God it's freezing. My mother bought two metal roll-around air conditioners, one for Carlos, Jr.'s room and one for mine. I hate the noisy thing and now my wet skin is all cold and clammy.

THE DREAM HAS bright overhead fluorescent lights. My cupped palm is above my brow but it's still difficult to see. I'm sitting in the kitchen, I'm positive of that. This is the Chicago apartment. Someone's here and I believe that person is Wren. She's at the gray and white flecked Formica counter near the sink with her back to me. Even under the brilliance of the fluorescent lights I recognize her clothes, the dark leather jacket, the skinny black jeans. Why won't she turn and look in my direction? Maybe she's mad or maybe she doesn't know I'm behind her. I begin calling to her but stop. I can't hear the words, not a breath. I feel my lips and tongue forming her name but that's it.

I start to get up from my seat at the white wood kitchen table but I can't do that, either. My legs are too heavy to move; I can't use my arms. Nothing works except my breathing. I feel panic rush hot through my chest. What's wrong with this place? What's wrong with me?

I don't know that I am dreaming, not then, not at that time, and I am very afraid I'm dead. Or that's my first thought, that I'm merely a spirit of myself sitting in a chair. I've become this pathetic spirit waiting for anybody to say hello.

C'mon and say *some*thing.

A hello. At least a hello.

I think Wren has turned to look at me. I want to shut off the lights. These lights don't illuminate, they blind. The metallic sparkle along the edges of Wren's narrow face must certainly be from the rows of tiny earrings.

"...Rhea?" she's saying. "Is it you, lovey?"

I have never heard Wren speak – that's obvious, I suppose. She is, after all, no more than an idea, a plotted thought. But I know how she'd sound, a south Philly girl, working class parents. I imagined her getting a steak and cheese at Pat's, on 9th and Wharton, having an occasional drink at Tony's Beef & Beer on East Oregon. "So yous wanna get beers at the Wawa?" But that's not what I hear. What I'm hearing is what people call Estuary English, an accent from South East England, London, south Essex, maybe Surrey. "How have you enjoyed this little talk?" *Howp youv injoid this littuw tawk?* It's that sort of accent.

"...Rhea?" she says again.

Who authorized this accent? I didn't, I had a South Philly girl. Tough, doesn't take shit. But she also has a good heart, she's loyal and your enemies are her enemies, that sort of person, the Wren I know, my Wren, my invention.

But then I get it.

My English father, born in Manchester. That's what Mother said. She'd said it more than once, so maybe it was true. They first met in London, Dr. Betty an undergrad student on vacation. My father worked for the *Guardian* then. Some photography, some reporting, as I understand it. Both of them were very young and very flattered by the interest of the other. It's my belief that Mother became infatuated more with Daddy's interest in her than with Daddy's looks or personality. Okay, I am sure that's unfair of me. The Dr. Betty part of Mother has said – and more than once – that I'm too sarcastic and cynical for my own good.

In my dream Wren is Father's girl, the very English side of things. I'm going to blame this on my psychotherapy, too. Here's the problem with therapy, a person thinks about too many uncomfortable things all at once. Dr. Allison says I'll feel worse before I start feeling better. In therapy the thoughts and feelings people avoid kick them like a hailstorm in Kansas.

I squint to get a better look. "...Wren?" That's what I try to say but her name comes out too soft and too distant.

"I can barely see you, lovey."

"I'm here, over here."

I'm waving my hand like a third grader wanting to use the bathroom. There is a cooked beefy smell in the kitchen, maybe hamburgers or steaks. Whatever, it was fried up awhile ago.

"Look what I have for you," Wren says. *Luk wha' I'ave faw yu.*

She's holding a thing in her hand but I don't know what the thing is, I can't see the lines of it. Then there's a flash, light inside of light. But the light Wren's holding is brighter than the light in the kitchen. Her hand folds about mine and I'm now clutching the black wood handle of a kitchen knife with a long serrated blade.

CARLOS, JR. IS sitting on the edge of my bed. He has on a sleeveless summer undershirt and jockey shorts and he looks entirely too skinny. Have I been feeding this boy? Are the two of us a bowl of frosted flakes away from malnutrition, a fast food-no food lifestyle? I'm sure Mother will rearrange our eating habits for the better. She's a huge health maniac, a vitamin, organic salad, fish and fowl person and I'm sure Carlos, Jr. and I will be healthy soon enough. No more cheese fries for breakfast. No more let's skip the next two meals because of last night's Twinkie marathon.

"Pick a card, Mama."

"...I'm too tired, baby."

"*Mama*. Pick a card."

Two-thirty in the morning and he has his deck of cards. He's going to entertain

me out of whatever craziness he thinks has taken his Mommy away from him and planet earth. Since Carlos, Sr. left us, it's become my darling child's S.O.P. to keep me tethered to him, his life's mission, his Don't-Let-Me Lose-Mommy-Too *modus operandi*. He's very good at card tricks and practices everyday. My son has Grandpa Lester's genes, I think.

I see him fine in the moonlight that crosses the wood floor and the bed. He's shuffling his cards. My sweet boy is tired, I can tell. I have not been good to my son. I haven't given him the peace of mind children need to get along in this world. Right now he is a weight on my shoulders and I pick a card because I feel I have to pick a card just as he offers the cards to me because he feels he has to do it. We are caught up in our love for one another and frozen in things we do not understand. We are lost to know what to do to bring the other one comfort.

IN MY DREAM Wren's face is very close to mine. I have drawn her this close many times but I've never been face to face with her, never so personally. The florescent light in the kitchen is intense and, even inches apart, her face is blurred by its brightness. Wren's small hands enfold my right hand, the one holding the knife. She begins to move my hand all the way up and all the way down. She does it over and over. As Wren does this, she's talking to me.

"...here's the way, lovey," she says.

"What do you mean?"

"Do it this way."

"Do what? What are you doing?"

"Us girls come down hard and straight. This is a must, I shouldn't have to say it.

We're that way from the start. Pretend you're sinking the knife into side of beef. Have you ever seen a butcher do the hard and straight? Their faces have no expressions and they come down and the knife goes into the beef like a pin into a soap bubble. *Pop!* It's what you do when you have a knife. We don't play around with it, we must go at it with our best. And no matter who you cut, you think of it as beef. Beef has no name, beef is dead before you start. That's how you should think. Understand, lovey? Whatever you cut and whatever you kill, it has no name."

"I don't cut people, I don't do that."

"It's not do or don't. It's when."

I shake my hand loose from her grip and toss the knife across the kitchen. It hits the back of the metal sink and skims over the floor and towards me. I want to be alone, away from Wren and her talk. But the knife is in my palm again and my fingers grip it again.

"We don't say no," Wren whispers.

Her hands press about my hand as if they had not left and I had not thrown the knife. I feel a damp heat coming off the black wood handle.

CARLOS, JR. IS asleep beside me in the bed. My sweat has become cold from the portable air conditioner. I look at Carlos and brush the hair from his forehead and I think about the older woman we met on the train from Chicago to Philly. She had short, curled white hair and too much rose perfume. The old lady was either on her cell phone or asleep and snoring. Her name was Miss Mona and she talked like we had known each other for years, best buds. Like I'd be in favor of that.

"Well Rhea dear, how does it feel to be a single mother?" I had shared a little of my recent life and I took what she said as code for "too bad you weren't a better wife." I realize I was probably being paranoid but she used that Holier Than Thou tone, as if she had the inside scoop on my life and didn't approve. Also, several minutes prior to the "single mother" thing, the woman made an indirect comment about my baby.

"So tell me," she'd said, "did you marry one of those Spaniard or some Filipino man?" Since when is my son's beautiful skin her business? At first I answered in my pathetically apologetic way but later I looked down at my book and keep quiet. Miss Mona did everything loud, she talked loud, slept loud, breathed loud. God. No wonder there was murder on the Orient Express.

"ARE YOU ALL right, Mama?"

Carlos, Jr. is looking up at me in the bed. It's funny. Not ha-ha funny, never that, but peculiar funny. The moonlight has turned his eyes silver. He is dark and thin and has a sleeveless white t-shirt and silver eyes.

"Can't you trust me?" I say. Of course he can't.

"I don't want you leaving, too."

"Where am I going to go? Realistically, where am I goin', the moon? A trip to Mars? Where?" I want to make light of this and show him it is his fear talking but I do not want

him thinking I'm making light of his feelings. Kids are difficult to love, to help. And I don't know what to do with him, the right thing to do, if there is a right thing. I just want to protect him the best I can, my sweet Carlos, and I would like to do it without driving us both crazy.

"Grandma says Daddy's scared of you."

"Daddy's just temporarily weird, baby. The man's six-foot-one and weighs what? Two hundred pounds? Two-fifty? Look at me, look at Mommy. I'm a Chihuahua. I'm maybe four pounds soaking wet. Who can hurt who, tell me? I'm more concerned about you. Are *you* scared of Mommy?"

"Sometimes. I'm scared when you don't act right."

"But I've *been* acting right. Haven't I? I've been okay."

"You tried to hurt him."

"Who said that? Did Grandma say that?"

He stays quiet.

THE STRONG LIGHT has not just bleached out the kitchen, the living room has the same look to it. I hate dreams that keep a person half blind. I can see only the outline of the sofa and the two chairs but not the patterns and not the colors. Carlos, Sr. got the furniture for our 21st wedding anniversary, the pieces have a silver background with tiny white blossoms. Very Japanesey. But most of this is lost to the light.

My dream doesn't want me to watch what goes on inside of it. That's what I'm beginning to believe. Since when have I become some type of frail flower that wilts at the sight of things? I'm denied the details of my what-you-call-it, my unconscious, my own creation. Something else. This is what I felt when I discovered the sketches. I'd walked into my studio and the sketches were waiting for me on the drawing board. But I couldn't see how I got from here to there. It's a feeling of being on the outside of who I am, of what I do.

Dr. Allison's treatment has not gone unnoticed by her patient.

"What're you planning?" Carlos, Sr. wants to know.

"I'm not planning anything."

"Go back in the kitchen with that."

"...with what?" I don't get what my husband's talking about or why he's so prickly. Why does he want me to go back to the kitchen? I was just *in* the kitchen. "What wrong with you?"

"Me? Nothing's wrong with *me*, okay? I'm fine, *I'm* dandy."

"You don't seem dandy."

"Oh I'm dandy. This man is going to have himself a life. A fuckin like *sane* life, okay? First time in twenty-God-knows-how-many years."

Our living room isn't that big and Carlos, Sr. isn't hard to miss. He's over six feet, his skin the color of teakwood. He's a formidable guy. But in this light he is not completely there.

"I can't give you a sane life?" I say. "When did this occur? *Twenty* years of suffering, what a brave soldier. Quick, somebody give him a medal."

"I'm glad you find this amusing."

"Please. Go have a sane life."

"How nice that my choices are all right with you." There is a quiver, a bravado to his voice. "I don't need your permission. This man's packed his bags, darlin'. Don't you go worrying yourself about this man."

I hadn't given any thought to this man and his "sane" life. None, zero, nada. And I'm not sure why. No, that's not true. I *know* why I didn't give it any thought. Less than five minutes ago Carlos, Sr. said he was leaving me for Ivy Landis and I had walked into the kitchen and promptly forgot. Like I'd been a drunk in a black out. I was fifteen when Carlos and I started talking, going out on dates, spending time together. He's the only man I've ever known – you know, in the biblical sense. So a person would think I could get to the kitchen and not forget stuff. Dr. Allison believes it was too important. "Too devastating," her exact words. But Now I'm remembering. And you know what? Fuck that Puerto Rican.

"You and Ivy *Landis*?" I can't believe it.

"It can't happen soon enough."

"That's so nuts."

"Hey. I'm not the one with the knife."

I look down at my hand and there is the kitchen knife with the black handle and the serrated blade. That's what's making him nervous. Good. Get nervous, you *puto*. And another thing, I'd be nervous about Ivy Landis, too. Nine chances out of ten, she's also got knives. And if you do this shit to me, you'll do it to her.

"You don't think I can't take that knife from you?" This is what my soon to be ex-husband says. He's got his swagger back but it's not all that genuine. "Don't worry, I'm not a stupid man, okay? I don't need going into a court and you telling the judge about a physical altercation, or whatever you call it. I'm not going down that road with you."

Maybe Carlos, Sr. was the one who installed these new lights, did it when I was doing other things. But how could that be? God there are too many mysteries and all I want is a place I can count on.

This light has taken away the exactness of things.

"Watch me, lovey." It's Wren.

She is standing on the sofa behind Carlos, Sr. I know her voice by now; I see the skinny legs wrapped in black jeans, the tiny bright metal earrings.

"Look here," she says.

Her feet are spread in a shoulder-wide stance, her clasped hands raised above her head. She begins a downward thrusting motion. Arms swing down then rise, down and rise. I start to do what she is doing. I raise my arms and swing them down. I watch her and copy that deep, downward thrust. I copy her noises, too. It's an *uhuh* sound as the knife goes from above my head to it's target below. *Uhuh*. The more I do the motion the easier it gets, the more rhythmic.

"The hard and straight," she says.

"The hard and straight," I say.

"Yes, keep doing that. Just like that."

Carlos, Sr. has stepped away. He's saying, "Stop it, Rhea! You hear? This is our furniture, for Christ-sake." I hear the panic now; I hear his arrogance start to go. "*Stop* it! This is crazy. I paid good money for that!" Bits of cloth and stuffing float about me and the constant swishing blade. White polyester batting powders my face, my arms, I even feel it on my eyelashes. While I'm doing this, there is a part of me standing away from it, an observer that does not want to believe what she is seeing. Is that me with a knife? A *knife*? Oh no, no. I would never *do* such a thing. This isn't what sweet Rhea Waye does. I'm mesmerized by the rise and the fall of the knife and the feel of sweat on my heated skin. Doing the hard and straight is exhausting work.

Carlos, Sr.'s voice has a whimper to it. "...please. Rhea? Hey hey. Come on, okay? All right?" The bullshit swagger has collapsed, that Puerto Rican hot shot crap. And he says again, "...hey...hey...c'mon now, Rhea. Hey. Rhea." Then he says, "Do you know how much that sofa cost?"

SEVEN

I TELL MYSELF I'm following Edward so he'll get home okay but I really just want to know where he lives. Or both – probably that and more – but certainly a little of both. I'm safe in saying that my reasons are complex. It's after 7:30 going on 8:00 and the evening is damp and warm and the sky still has some pink threaded in it. Tonight I decided to carry my large black canvas handbag. I've a ham and cheese sandwich on rye in there, along with a few other things. I've also asked Mother to watch Carlos, Jr. for awhile. Of course she loved that idea. Anytime Mother can be alone with my son she'll take it.

God knows what she says about me.

Earlier in the day I'd questioned Sister Kathrin at Little Sisters of Mercy about the man with the cane who visited on Mondays and she said, "Edward, I think. His name is Edward." I've made a point of being friendly toward Sister Kathrin. I believe the sister likes me as much as I like her but she refused to give me the man's last name because of "confidentiality issues." Who knows if his name is even Edward. People will make up anything. You know how that goes.

Edward takes the Broad Street subway at City Hall going north toward the Broad and Eire stop, about a fifteen minute ride. It's all underground and the windows are dark except for an occasional passing yellow light and the cars have a steel-and-creak sound and everything trembles. You can't escape the smell, either. Some days and some cars are worse than others. It depends on who did what to whom or who did what to the car. Vomit, piss, too much disinfectant, it's up to the car and the chance you take. This evening it's a potpourri.

"SO YOU'RE LETTING yourself remember?"

"It was a dream."

"But it's very close to what you're mother said to me." Dr. Allison is reviewing pages from her notebook. Previous sessions, maybe, I don't know. "Not with Wren and all of that, of course. What your husband told her – the knife, the furniture, those sort of things. It's why she thought he sounded frightened." Then Allison looks at me. "What happened next?"

"I dropped the knife and ran."

"That's when you were hit by the cab?"

"...yes."

I don't notice that I'm crying, not immediately, this is how out of it I am. Who doesn't notice that? But I start to feel my eyes burn and the heat on my cheeks. I touch the outside corner of my left eye with a fingertip and rub the wetness between my thumb and forefinger. I look down at the tears as if they come from a stranger.

"Talk about what you're feeling," Dr. Allison says.

"I don't know what I'm feeling."

"I think you do."

Her office has that same clean and measured look, session after session, the rugs, the leather furniture, the empty white walls. Her perfume is measured too, never any less, never any more.

Why do I share myself and she doesn't? It seemed unfair at first but this isn't a friendship, I know that now. We're not buddies, we don't go out for a coffee. We don't text or follow each other on Twitter or go to the movies. Not that Dr. Allison isn't a nice person. Or as friendly as circumstances will allow, I guess. She isn't above a smile or a kind tone to her words. This is a treatment, though, and I am its star, its one and only, and there are sessions when I like that idea and there are sessions when it just plain shits. I'm the sort of person who needs a few shadows handy, a nearby place to go and hide. Here the spotlight won't quit.

"Talk, please. Don't miss the opportunity."

I'm not sure how to put it or why I should feel the way I do but I say it anyhow. "I'm scared for Carlos, Jr.," I tell her, and somewhat defensively. "Okay? Is that fine with you? I'm scared for my son."

I AM ROUGHLY a half-block behind Edward. The street lamps are on and the sky is dark but clear and full of stars and there is a quarter moon. This area of North Philadelphia is called Nicetown. It's an older part of the city with lots of brick and white wood row houses that date back to the thirties and forties, some older than that. Most houses have tiny porches and tiny front yards and practically every house has a tree or two and a tall shrub. Boxwood, I'm thinking. Working people live here, most people have more than one job if they can get it. But jobs are scarce now and people are frightened.

Edward must be in his sixties but slim and elegant in his gabardine. I imagine him being the maître de at a fancy Center City restaurant or maybe a concierge at some little boutique hotel in Rittenhouse Square. And for a man with a cane, his gait is crisp, unflagging.

I have no reason to follow Edward, certainly nothing logical. But I quit my visit with Grandpa Lester thirty minutes early to just to wait for him. I stood by a newsstand close to the Little Sisters of Mercy, ready to stalk the guy. Like I'm a thirteen years old waiting for a rock star – well maybe not that. I have no sexual feelings for him, or none that I am aware of, but there is a feeling of urgency.

Wait. I am not being completely honest.

With Edward I've allow myself to picture my father. Not that I think Edward *is* my father. It's more that he let's me think about him, what he might be like today, his appearance, his manner. I also believe this new insistence to imagine Father has to do with my divorce, the suddenness of losing Carlos, Sr. Maybe Dr. Allison is right, one loss let's us think about and mourn other losses. But it's not that I've stumbled upon my father in his elder years. We not talking about that line in *Casablanca,* "...of all the gin joints, in all the towns, she walks into mine." I can see serious men in long white coats coming for me at the mere whisper of that one.

"DID YOU EVER see film of the Thailand tsunami? 2004, I think?" I've leaned not to wait for Dr. Allison to answer my questions. Most of the time she likes to hear me for awhile before she talks. Or that's what she says, anyway. "I saw a documentary of it on TV. This little boy was playing on the beach near the water's edge. But there's no water. The ocean had retreated from the beach. I mean fishing boats were on their sides, Fish flopping around. Is this all right to talk about? You said to talk about whatever comes to mind."

"Let's see where it goes." Dr. Allison's writing notes again and doesn't look up.

"I'm taking you at your word."

"...go on."

"Okay, well. That's what happens first in a tsunami, it's like the ocean takes a hike, literally. The little boy I saw playing on the beach couldn't have been more than four or five. A baby, you know? No shirt, black hair, very tan. Then the wave is coming – actually it's a giant wall, a giant blue wall – but the boy doesn't see it, he's not paying attention. I mean kids, what're you going to do, right? They're oblivious, these kids. And don't ask me where the stupid mother is. God only knows. Shooting crack, I don't know. And this wave is coming, this blue wall, we can see it. The biggest damn thing you can imagine. But the little boy's unaware, totally in left field. He's squatting to check something out in the sand and this wave – this blue wall the size of a three story building, easy – this big-ass thing, it slams down on him and he's gone. *Poof!* I mean *gone*, seriously gone. As in no-fucking-more. Like that," I say and snap my thumb against my forefinger. "Can you imagine?"

"...awful." Dr. Allison shakes her head but she doesn't stop writing.

"Somebody's sweet little boy. This poor kid, you know? And the poor mother and father. Imagine the guilt. If that had been my Carlos, Jr., I couldn't bear the guilt. What the hell do you do? How does a person keep on living? Oh my son died, let's go shopping, let's go to the movies. Know what I mean? Who does that? And maybe the kid had, you know, a brother or a sister. Then you'd have to deal with their feelings. So the whole family's crazy and who knows for how long. Talk about a nightmare."

"We never know what's going to happen when, do we?" Dr. Allison guides a strand of her gray hair behind her ear with her fingertips. Her hair is very short and neat but she still likes fussing with it. "You mentioned that..." She looks down at her notes and flips back a page. "...you were scared for your son?"

"...I did?"

"Maybe twenty minutes ago, yes."

Dr. Allison and I are sitting in identical dark leather chairs across from each other.

I'm looking beyond her shoulder at nothing in particular. My mind is suddenly empty. It's the nothingness before the Big Bang. Then I finally get a thought, *did I really say that?* And another, *Am I frightened for my son?*

At first I don't remember then I do.

"It's that little boy on the beach. You think he's Carlos, Jr.?"

"Maybe something you think, that he'll be swept away?"

I feel heat welling up about my throat and behind my eyes. This time I do feel the tears. I see my son as helpless, he is a boy with no father and half a mother and that half has too many wacky days. I don't know how to protect him from this life. Some days from me. How do I teach him? I don't know how to protect myself, there are too many uncontrollable things. You know the Serenity Prayer recovering alcoholics say, that stuff about accepting the things you can't change? Well guess what, the fucking things that surprise us are the very things we can't change.

EDWARD LIVES IN one of the West Hunting Park row houses, the brick and white wood deals with the small gray porches and the tree and the over grown boxwood.

These row house are more rundown than others I've seen. Fresh paint is needed, his front door screen should be patched or replaced. The boxwood has a raggedy look. His lawn is more gray dirt than grass. A few new shingles wouldn't hurt, either. I'd pictured Edward living in a less tacky place.

It's dark now and I've been standing on his porch for close to an hour. There are street lamps but nothing close enough to interfere with my shadows. The window shade is raised slightly and I can see Edward watching the TV. It's a game show, I'm guessing, though I'm not altogether sure. I see people singing and other people talking to them after they've finished their song. Judges? Who knows, I don't watch much TV. Edward is wearing a black and pale blue striped bathrobe and black slippers with white socks and his skinny legs are just as white as the socks.

I'm terribly disappointed in him. Who knows what I expected but I didn't expect this. My God. I refuse to believe he's such a tedious old man. There are other and more valid scenarios. Perhaps he must hide his true identity. And why not? Some people are unwilling to reveal themselves. They'd be in danger if they did so, especially those who have lived clandestine lives. Those who've put themselves into one risky situation after another and simply aren't satisfied with nine to five. Spies, perhaps. Or people who've cooperated with federal agencies to bring the more devious of us to justice. It's obvious, doesn't this happen all the time? Can you, for example, imagine my father going from being a photojournalist in the Yom Kippur war to having skinny white legs and watching a TV game show? I think not. But he might do it as a ploy, a disguise, a way to lure or escape the criminal element. If my father had succumbed to such a life, he would have told the black ugly birds in the desert to come on and eat the buffet. And be quick about it. These aren't men who do such things. These are the *crème dela crème*, the big dogs, the movers and shakers, the masters of whatever universe suits them.

No. No robes and TV for these boys.

"DO YOU TRULY believe this man is your father?"

"I've never stalked anybody in my life," I say, dodging Dr. Allison's question. "That's not me. Well it's certainly *me* but it's never been me before last night. If I were to stalk a man, I'd like him to be somewhere in my ballpark. Generationally, I mean."

"This isn't about dates."

"It's a joke. God you're so serious."

"What would you have done with him?" She ignores the humor. "Say you meet him, then what? Is there a plan?"

"I-I hadn't thought that far ahead," I tell her. I'm looking at the empty white wall again, the one to my right.

"Oh I disagree. I think you know. Most people have a plan, a fantasy. They may not act on it. It may not be in the forefront of the mind, at least not in the beginning. But it's there."

"Not everyone's the same."

"You'd be surprised."

I don't know how I got into all of this but I want to get out of it. I'm feeling too comfortable with Dr. Allison, always ordering me to say what comes to mind. And my thoughts come out before I have a chance to examine them. I'm beginning to believe everything in this office is designed to get a person to talk, to stir a person up, to confess secrets. The lighting is perfect, the temperature – I never sweat in here – but mostly it's Dr. Allison's attitude. She has that thing going on. She is the snake charmer and I am the snake being charmed.

IT HAS BEEN at least an hour, or feels like it. I am still crouched on Edward's porch, hiding in the night and in shadows laid by the moon and the corner street lamp. Yes, spying on him. My knee joints are aching and the night is too hot, too humid. I feel hungry and stupid. To be honest, I'm also worried about the conversations that Mother and Carlos, Jr. might be having. I don't know how bad Mother's innuendos and so on will be and what repair work I'll have to do once

I'm home. Laugh if you will, the two of them are unbelievable and Carlos, Jr. comes away from these get-togethers with a lot of phony-baloney information. But I am here and don't want to leave. I'm looking through the bottom part of the window, the part not blocked with the shade. Edward is sitting in his chair, a green felt recliner, and his feet are propped up and crossed at the ankles. His robe has fallen away from his legs and the legs are thinner and whiter than I'd originally thought. I'm not sure what he's watching on TV. Men with guns, I think. And when the men are not showing each other their guns, they are chasing each other in their cars.

My black canvas handbag is starting to cut into my shoulder and I put the black bag beside me. Then I think about the sandwich, the ham and cheese on rye I'd tossed into the bag before I left to visit Lester at the Little Sisters of Mercy, a zip-locked and fresh sandwich. Can a person eat and spy? I don't have a clue. Maybe there's a protocol, some social thing I am not privy to. I'm figuring spy work is different than a stakeout. In a stakeout you have a car and nobody notices you. People buy donuts at a stakeout, an Italian sub.

This is how I amuse myself.

But then I look down at the open canvas bag and I'm not amused. I don't get it, why don't I get *anything*? It's the story of my current life, my hideous fate, not to get a damn thing.

In the bag there is a good twenty feet of clothesline rope, that's what we used to call it, Mother and I, that hard white rope. It's wrapped very neatly, very precisely. I also see a new roll of duct tape, a folded handkerchief and a small amber bottle. The label on the bottle reads "Chloroform, 500 ML." Beneath these things is my serrated kitchen knife.

EIGHT

SISTER KATHRIN AND I are eating lunch in a neighborhood bar called Tommy Noel's. Tommy's has dark wood booths and dark walls and the booths have red leather seats. There are photos on the walls and Sister Kathrin says the photos are of a few local singers who didn't do that well and old Philadelphia politicians. The place is on Locust Street where Grandpa Lester stays at the Little Sister's of Mercy. We're having luscious heart attack burgers with Vidalia onion, tomato and lettuce on buttery grilled buns. There are also Diet Pepsis in large Styrofoam cups and side orders of hot and salty fries.

"I'm sure this is a sin," the sister says.

"...want something else?"

"I'm kidding. Eat."

Sister Kathrin is the tiniest of all the Little Sisters. She's a three-foot-two thirty year old who wears a black floor length habit and a head cover that frames her round face in white. Her glasses have thick lenses and magnify very blue eyes. Right now my urge is to pick her up and sit her on my lap. I want to feed Sister Kathrin my burger and give her lots of big hugs. I keep reminding myself that this is a grown woman with a Master of Divinity from Duquesne.

"Every time I see Edward I think about Daddy." I say this as I'm eating one of my fries and I have to cover my mouth with the flat of my hand as I talk.

"...who's that?"

"Edward. The man with the cane?" Nothing sparks in her. "He visits the patient in the room with my grandfather – the one behind the curtain?"

"Many patients are behind curtains."

"You said his name was Edward."

Sister Kathrin is looking at me but she has no expression. A second or two pass before her face comes alive and it comes alive in sections. First her eyes remember the man. This is followed by a quick a smile and, lastly, a nod.

"He visits the boy," she says. At last, recognition

"The patient is a boy?"

"Eleven, maybe twelve. I forget, exactly. He was in bad shape when he came to us. I shouldn't talk too much about him. Confidentiality and so on, people are very particular on what we can and can't say about patients."

"Now I'm curious. "

"Sorry I don't mean to tease."

"Tell me what you can," I say. I'm still unnerved by last night on Edward's porch and the rope and knife I "found" in my black canvas bag. Any clue that might allow me to feel less nuts would be helpful.

"Well I can talk about these *type* of cases, that sort of thing."

"Whatever's comfortable," I tell her.

"Nothing about this is comfortable. There are people in the world who treat other people, very helpless people, like animals." Her voice is hesitant, more emotional. "I've gone into homes to rescue children. Adults, too. Not alone, of course, I don't go alone but I have gone into places. I've seen people in dog collars, people chained to walls and posts. There is an odor to these...places, a foulness. Children kept in basements, elderly people. Many are malnourished and naked. Skin with blisters, lacerations, bruises, you don't want to know. Some with big welts, where they were whipped or kicked, or who knows what. It's horrible to see what I've seen. Like going into hell. It's horrible to see the way we treat each other."

CARLOS, JR. SITS on his bed with his thin tanned legs crossed Indian style. One of Mother's shoeboxes is next to him – I'm guessing it's hers – and letters and photos are spread around.

"What's going on?" I want to know. I'd arrived home late from my lunch with Sister Kathrin, about twenty minutes after the school bus had dropped off my son. I feel terrible, I always want to be home for him. "Hey Mommy's talking to you, Carlos."

"...letters and pictures." He reading and doesn't look up.

I sit on the edge of the bed near him and kiss his cheek and look at one of the photos. "Okay, what do we have here?" I say.

"Your daddy."

I haven't seen these pictures in thirty-some years. Tears flood my vision and take hot trails down my cheeks. This is Jeffery David Waye – J.D. himself. In one picture he's standing in the desert, slim and young and holding his Nikon F Photomic FTN under his right arm. He wears sunglasses and his khaki pants match the shirt. Draped about his head is a white keffiyeh.

The English love to play dress up.

"Mama? Are you all right?"

"...fine, baby. Just surprised."

I'm tempted to sit here with my son and look at the photos and read the letters but I am already getting anxious just thinking about it and I don't know why, exactly. I think I like the vagueness. Once you get your history straight – what follows what – you can't change it anymore, there's just no wiggle room.

Carlos, Jr. is studying my face. The boy stays worried. "Grandma says you and her used to look at these pictures all the time." He inches over to the edge of the bed and sits next to me and loops his arm about mine. "She says you were little then, younger than I am now."

"I was a baby – four, maybe five."

"...you all right? I don't want you sick again."

"I know." Best not to tell him about last night, my campout on Edward's porch with my black canvas gift bag.

MY TIME WITH Sister Kathrin has stayed with me. At the end of our lunch Tommy Noel's was empty except for sister and me in our dark booth and an older man sitting at the bar. The man was hunched over a beer while he watched the Phillies playing somebody on the small TV and the bartender stood near the man but on the opposite side of the bar and watched the game off and on as he cleaned whiskey glasses with the edge of his apron.

"Being a little person has lots of health issues," Sister Kathrin said. We'd been talking about this. It was inevitable, I suppose. "Particularly joint and back problems, those are two big ones. I don't want to tell you the amount of surgeries I've had – spine, legs, hips. Especially hips. You name it, I've gone through it. But between that, I live my life and I try not to think about it."

"Is that possible?"

"No. But if I help somebody else, I think less about myself. I'm not a selfless person, believe me. I help others so I can survive."

Sunlight came through front glass window and slanted yellow and dusty over the mahogany bar. The

people on the TV and the bartender and the old man
with the beer were cheering. I'd guessed the Phillies got
a run.

"Can I talk to you about Edward?"

"You can talk. I may not answer."

"Is the boy his son? His grandson?"

"A nephew, his brother's boy. The brother died four
months ago and the boy went to live with the uncle."

"You mean Edward."

"His Uncle Edward, yes. The judge had asked the
nephew what he wanted to do and the boy chose his
uncle." Sister Kathrin pressed her clear plastic framed
glasses to the bridge of her nose with her middle finger.
The magnified lenses had enlarged her eyes and the
eyes looked too big for her face. "I'm going to feel
uneasy beyond this point," she said. "Talking about the
boy, I mean. I know you have questions but as long he's
a patient with us I need think about privacy issues. But
let me ask you a question."

"Whatever you'd like."

"Why Edward? This fascination."

"I'm not sure I'm ready to answer that. I'm not sure
I know, actually. Perhaps both of us can only go so far
with this."

How do I discuss an obsession?

I am sure Dr. Allison is right, one loss in our lives
probably does give us a second chance to mourn other
losses. Particular a father, *my* father, what loss is
bigger to a little girl? Had I come across Edward at a
different time in my life I wouldn't have given him a
thought. But things are what they are and I don't know
how to stop the fascination, if it is that – nor do I want
to stop it. Play it through, I say, let it go where it will go.
There is something to be said for that sort of approach.
Find out what it is I want and why I want it. Dr. Allison
agrees with me. But she'd like me to find it – whatever

"it" is – in therapy with her. "Talk it out, don't act it out," she forever says. It's her mantra. I say who cares where or how I find it.

Does Edward have chains in his basement, dog collars? Did his brother? That's what I'm wondering, that's what got my attention. Why would Sister Kathrin say that? Never speak in generalities to someone like me. What I can weave with a generality is stunning. I don't even have to try, it comes automatically.

Imagine the nephew at age four, at five or six. He wears a leather dog collar and a chain is hooked from the collar to a ceiling or a wall, a long chain. The child can walk to the dark corners of the basement or walk halfway up the stairs to get a tray of food. No one bothers the boy and not to be bothered is a blessing. He doesn't want these parents bothering with him. They are always angry. They kick him and whip him and think he's a curse. How dare he fuck up their lives, how dare he breathe, how dare he exist. The boy is a mistake and the parents are too dumb to do anything about the mistake except to keep the boy as a sport for their unyielding rage.

They rarely give him fresh clothes; they don't bathe him, either. The basement floor is hard gray dirt and the boy's piss and shit keep accumulating and the floor must be hosed down once a week or the smell becomes too strong. They also get mad about that. But the boy is strong and has good DNA or maybe he has an anger that lets him survive, or both. Or perhaps he is simply a child favored by God.

What I can weave with a generality is stunning.

MY SON AND I are still sitting next to each other on the edge of his bed. We're looking at pictures of my father and reading his letters. Late afternoon sunlight is coming through the slats of the Venetian blinds and across the bedspread and the polished wood floor. I have read three of my father's letters but it's the fourth one that I have read more than once. It's like an old timey record needle stuck in a bad grove. Click-click. Repeat. Click-click. Repeat.

Darling Betty,

The desert nights are good for dreaming but the dreams aren't very good. Maybe it's the emptiness of the place, or the cold and the darkness of it, or maybe it's being away from you. But I am up now and wide awake from the latest my latest dream.

This is how it starts. My leg is wounded and I am laying on my back and the sun is hot on my face and chest and the sand has my blood on it.

Think of that! The sand and the blood. And yes, my dream gets worse from there. The pain from the wound is God-awful and I keep fainting and waking and faint again.

The dream is an overdone version of the wound I had received a month ago. The very leg! Of course the wound in my dream was far more flamboyant – a machine gun ripping the flesh. In my waking life, it had been a single bullet from a rifle. Painful enough, believe me.

You have married a lunatic, my darling.

Oh the best part are the birds. Where I got these birds from I will never know. A complete fabrication. I want to call them vultures but they are too big for that. Tall and skinny with black feathers and scarlet faces and white beaks: unnerving creatures, really. Golden eyes.

The birds perch on the rocks and the sand and more of them gather during the day. These big ugly things watch me but keep their distance. I know they are hungry and I know they are waiting for me to die.

See what being away from you does?

It gives me the creeps just writing...

Click-click. Repeat.

This is a mini revelation. My God. This is more about my mother's thinking than my father's dream. Throughout my life Mother has referred to me as "Walter Mitty in patent leather shoes." She's very serious about the Walter Mitty thing and I've always thought it was hilarious. Now I have a letter from my father saying he *had* been wounded but by a bullet. But it was from a *rifle* and not the raging *rat-a-tat* machine gun fire of his dream.

What's fascinating is Mother. *She loved Daddy's dreams better than his day to day.* Multiple wounds from a machine gun, large dark birds waiting for him to die, that's what I had been told, what I grew up hearing. Her bedtime stories about him remind me of how kids talk about ghosts around a summer campfire. No wonder my life is always in the throws of fantasy. My parents provided me with a career. Mother had a thing for Daddy's adventures, his Lawrence of Arabia outfits, his *dreams*. In my family, Walter Mitty could have been any of us.

"...you all right?" Carlos, Jr. is asking this again.

I drop my father's letter into the shoebox behind me on the bed and wrap an arm about my son's far too skinny shoulders, my forehead resting on his soft dark hair.

"Why did grandma give you this stuff," I whisper.

"I don't know," he says and shrugs.

The boy is looking at pictures of a young J.D. Waye in his Lawrence of Arabia outfit. Carlos doesn't want to get involved in mother-daughter hassles. Who can blame him? I hate the hassles, too. But it doesn't prevent me from pumping him for whatever information he's keeping a secret.

"I know you two talk," I say.

He stays quiet, examining the photos.

"Carlos, Mother's speaking."

"I don't *know*."

My son wants to do the right thing but he's finding out early on that the right thing is usually vague and complicated and will inevitably hurt somebody.

"I should share." He delivers these words like a confession. "With you. I should share the letters and the pictures with you."

"Grandma said that?"

"She says you invent things."

"*I* invent things?" I feel an arching eyebrow coming on. "Oh *really*."

"But you can't help it."

"Poor me."

"It's not funny."

"I agree, baby. Believe me."

My mother stopped the bedtime stories about my father because I liked to correct her. Or better, make up my own stories. *It didn't happen that way, Mommy,* I'd say. *It happened this way.* And I would take off on some tangent or other. It usually involved a man from the desert saving a little girl from an evil stepmother. Yada yada yada. You know how a kid can get – stubborn, an ungrateful Little Miss.

"...you need a reality check," Carlos, Jr. is saying.

"Well somebody here needs something."

He's become a miniature Dr. Betty. It's like listening to one annoying person but in stereo. I will admit that seeing my father's photographs and reading his letters have stirred undefinable feelings inside me; also physical things. The physical stuff is in my chest and in my arms. Literally, a trembling. Or a sort of rocky unsteadiness, as if I am being detached from the ground.

I'm beginning to think Mother has arranged all of

this, bless her well-intended heart – coming here to Philadelphia, the appointments with Dr. Allison. Now we have the *piece de resistance*, the letters and photographs of my father. Sweet, isn't? When you think about it, what could be sweeter?

Mother is trying to save me.

A BLUE AND white is parked at the Locust Street entrance to the Little Sisters of Mercy. Sister Kathrin and I are walking back from Noel's and we're both watching the two police officers. The guys are waist-high in five or six of the sisters and everybody's talking at once. Black habits and long white head coverings whip and curl in the warm afternoon breeze.

"This is the way it is," Sister Kathrin says. To herself, mostly.

"What way's that?"

"I go out to lunch and I get this."

"You mean a reprimand from the Lord?"

"I mean frantic women."

A patient has escaped, the boy Edward visits, the nephew. Or that's what I'm gathering. Sister Kathrin is now trying to calm the other sisters but they have things to say and points to make and nobody is listening to anybody.

"Is this a court order?" One of the cops says this to Kathrin. He's a good six feet and his rust colored hair is too thick for his hat. "Can you calm these people down?" His voice gets louder, "Did a judge *order* the patient to this facility?"

"He's voluntary," Sister Kathrin says. She turns to the other sisters and puts a forefinger to her lips and the sisters actually stop talking.

"How is this our problem?" The other cop wants to know. He's just as tall as the one with the bad hair but maybe ten years younger and a lot slimmer. "Does he need certain edications? Is this a life or death thing, what?"

I'm listening as Sister Kathrin begins talking about Edward's nephew. Michael. That's the boy's name – Michael. And she's saying, no. no. It's not that. It's not a life or death situation, not in the way the two patrolmen mean.

While they are talking I remember Carlos, Jr. telling me about going behind the curtain in Grandpa Lester's room. What I'd been doing at that moment I don't know, I'm never in the right place at the right time or doing the right thing.

Where was the mother, that's what I imagine people saying. *Doesn't this woman care about her child? Doesn't she ever pay attention?*

I think I was looking at Grandpa Lester's scrapbook with him.

"That's a handsome woman," he'd said.

"That's Vera. Your wife."

"I'm married to *that*?"

"She's passed on, Grandpa."

"...my luck."

This is our standard twice weekly conversation. But I also believe I remember seeing Carlos, Jr. disappear behind the curtain. I know he'd read Michael's chart, that's what my son confessed, and he had placed his phone number under the boy's pillow.

I should have listened better.

Sister Kathrin is talking to the two officers but she isn't looking at the men or the other nuns. Her small right hand is cupped above her brow to block the sun. She glances at the front of Mercy's three story brown brick building and the sidewalk – a sweeping right to left view – then the afternoon traffic. What Sister Kathrin looks at last she looks at the longest. It's the Walnut-Locust subway entrance at the corner.

NINE

"WHY AM I always the villain?"

"Who else do I have?"

"Everything's a joke, isn't it?" Dr. Betty is in her therapist mode this morning, sipping coffee at the kitchen table. She's wearing the pale green kimono with the pink cherry petals and her legs are crossed at the knee. "What's wrong with you and the boy reading a few letters and looking at some pictures? The man is your father – or was."

"You've decided he's dead?"

"He's dead to me."

"We don't know that," I say. I start washing my breakfast dish at the sink and looking out the window. "People are supposed to get notified, a certificate or phone call. He had a driver's license, right? Dental records, DNA. Disappearing isn't easy.

Grandpa Lester used to tell us that all the time. He'd say, 'Listen, hon, disappearing is a tough trick.' Don't you remember him saying that?"

"Your grandfather *did* tricks for a living," Mother says. "Your father isn't in our lives and he hasn't been in our lives for years. Be sensible. Do you really believe he'll just show up one day, knock on the door?"

This morning started before the sunlight, before my argument with Mother in the kitchen. Okay, the word "argument" won't do. We'll call it a discussion, a differing of opinions. One opinion is very sane and rational. The other opinion is my mother's.

I WAKE UP worrying about my boy, how little I have to offer him. I walk into the studio, switch on the white flex-neck lamp attached to the drawing board and begin sketching. For a minute or two I can't get enough air into my lungs and my hand has a tremor. But the more I draw the calmer I become, it's like that with me.

Wren is running across the rooftops and Carlos, Jr. is with her. Moonlight goes through the clouds and the darkness with long threads of silver. I'm using a pencil to draw one quick piece after the other and I imagine the colors, the details and the motion of Wren and my son. She has on the leather jacket, her skinny black jeans, her hightops.

"You have to keep up," Wren says. What I'm imagining her saying. She has turned to watch Carlos but she doesn't quit her stride. It's become a backpedal sort of run. Wren grabs the boy's arms and pulls him along. "How are you going to get by in this world? You have no endurance."

"I'm tired, I don't *like* running."

"You can't be tired whenever it suits you."

I'm drawing my boy stoop-shouldered, one foot landing flat in front of the other, an exhausted Carlos, Jr. He's weary from this training he never wanted but must have to survive.

As I draw I'm starting to hear that Dinner Music Quartet from my Chicago days in the background – as if it's on the radio, distance and barely audible – the two violins, the clarinet, the grand piano. It's Cole Porter's "Anything Goes." I don't know where it's coming from but I never do. My anxiousness has returned and the music doesn't help.

Wren leaps off the edge of the rooftop, dropping through shadow and light onto another one several yards below. Carlos, Jr. is standing above her, looking down.

"Get on with it," Wren says in that British accent. "Do it now. Jump."

I sketch my son in mid-air, his legs spread, his arms over his head. He's

very wide-eyed and his mouth is open in a pantomimed scream.

"*That's* it," she's saying, arms open for him.

In the next sketch Wren has caught the boy and allows herself to fall backwards with Carlos on top of her.

"You're very brave, lovey."

"I-I was scared."

"That's all right. That's perfectly fine, everybody gets scared." Wren is kneeling in front of my son, brushing the knees of his jeans. "It's not how you feel. It's what you do."

I want Carlos, Jr. strong but I'm not sure what he needs to get strong. What do people need to work their lives, to sidestep the shocks and the disappointments, to endure? There's nothing I can find in my repertoire to help him and I can't let what's happened to me happen to my son. Life is crazy enough without getting crazy with it. Why must I pass on the fear and the anger that I can't give a face to, that confuses me? It's like a dowry of faded paintings. Or Snake Pit genes. What a lovely fucking inheritance for a kid. Here's my psyche, sweetheart, but just stay away from sharp objects. Carlos must learn to do the things I don't know to how teach him, things I don't know how to do myself. I want to help my boy to look at the world and see what is there and know what is not there.

"YOU'RE CONCERNED ABOUT me," I say.
"Well I'm your mother."

"But you're concerned. We're talking major concern. Am I right?" I can't get over this. Why I have the creeps about it, I don't know. But I feel terribly uncomfortable. My stomach has a knot in it the size of a fist. I'm not used to Mother freaking out on me in a protective way. I need her calm, I need her in control. *It's just my foolish daughter, you know how she is —* that sort of thing.

I need Mother to think I'm okay or at least that I'll *be* okay.

"Is there's a law against me being concerned?"

"But this isn't simply an 'I'm your mother' concern. Like eat your veggies

or clean your room – Mother concerns. See this is about how I scared the shit out of you and my-soon-to-be ex."

"You cut up your furniture with a kitchen knife." Mother whispers this like it's a secret. She's holding her coffee cup with both hands and watching the steam rise. "You ran out of the apartment and got hit by a taxi."

"I'm aware, thank you."

"Excuse me. Who brought this up?"

"I want to know why. It's a legitimate question."

"I love you, Rhea. You're my daughter, my only child. Of course I have a major concern?"

I also hate it when Mother becomes logical. I know what you're thinking, *Here's a mother who can't win. If she doesn't care, the daughter feels neglected. If she does care, the daughter feel uncomfortable. Even a little crazy.* But what's true is this: when Mother becomes logical I have to become *as* logical or *more* logical just to appear sane – just to break even.

How come nobody gets that?

"The Puerto Rican thinks it's the divorce." Ah Dr. Betty, psychologist of the airwaves.

"His name is Carlos."

"Whatever." Mother has a sip of coffee and makes a face at it. She adds a second teaspoon of sugar, stirs it and has another sip. "You met him when? You were ten, twelve, what?"

"Real close. Fifteen."

"You always acted like a little girl with him. You used to do the baby talk thing. Do you remember that, the baby talk thing?"

"I don't baby talk." Actually, I do. Or did.

"Don't tell me I'm wrong," Mother says and looks up from her coffee and graces me with eye contact. Once she gets ahold of something the woman is like one of those suction fish on a shark. Then she says, "You know exactly what I'm talking about, Rhea. He's tall. He's strong. He can beat people up. That Puerto Rican is what little girls who never had a father think a father *should* be. The protector, the knight in armor deal."

"...oh God."

"Laugh if you want."

"I'm not laughing."

"You used to look for your father in every man on street. I can still hear you doing it. 'Isn't that Daddy?' you'd say. Or, 'Look at that man over there, Mama. Does he look like Daddy?' You'd do it all the time. Or I'd find you talking to some stranger. It's a wonder you weren't kidnapped."

"What can I say? I missed not having a father."

"I think you were heartbroken. And furious."

"I don't know about furious."

"Oh I do, it's true. Abso*lute*ly."

"It's too early to argue, Mother."

I was five or so the last time my father and I were together. The two of us had gone to the Philadelphia Zoo. And there was a cane involved, too. A wooden cane. So this was directly after the Yom Kippur war.

I can see my father sitting on a bench near a chain link fence and, beyond that, an enormous gray wrinkled elephant. Trees shadow my father's face, his bad leg stiffly set in front of him. I'm hobbling around with his cane, pretending I'm a little crippled girl. I make war noises and toss the cane in the air and fall down and clutch my knee.

"Want a pretzel?" Daddy says.

"I need a medic." I swear I remember saying that.

In the morning before we went to the zoo, my father talked about the medics with mother and me while we ate pancakes with blueberries and whip cream. This has always been my father's favorite food. He said the medics could sew up a leg or an arm even if people were shooting at them. My mother told him this got her way too emotional and fluttered her fingers at her eyes so her mascara wouldn't run. She told him if he kept that up he'd have a raccoon for a wife.

I HAVEN'T LEFT my drawing board but I've been thinking more than drawing, particularly about the conversation I had yesterday with Sister Kathrin. I could never do what she does, go into those houses, see the sort of things she has seen, the neglect, the violence. I cannot envision her having a peaceful sleep. Or any sleep at all, really. Imagine the images: young ones and old ones collared and chained in the darkness. I've never seen any of it and I can already picture the dirt and sores on their skin, the stench of them.

I wish I hadn't asked about Edward and his nephew Michael. Isn't that his name? Michael, the tortured. Michael, the escapee. Now I have an entire fantasy concocted and it's disturbing. My fantasy is probably closer to what's real than I'd care to admit. I gravitate toward people who've been abused by disinterest, the dumped, the forsaken, it's in my DNA.

Dr. Allison has said as much; and though I hate to admit it, Dr. Betty has also had a few insights.

I'm looking through the sketches I drew earlier this morning. The sun has started to rise and there is some gold and pink in the sky and the light is relieving the shadows. Then I realize I don't remember drawing the last five sketches. I go back and look at the pictures again, slower this time.

In the first sketch the man with the cane is sprawled on a dirt floor. It's a basement, I think. His cane lays to the left of him. Lines and shading are dark and done in a hurried way. Wren and Carlos, Jr. squat beside him. My son holds a cloth and a small bottle. It's very much like the bottle of chloroform I had in my black canvas bag. The next sketch has Wren binding the man's ankles with rope. This scene is followed by another showing Wren and my son pulling the rope and the man lifting off the dirt floor feet first.

The last two sketches are almost identical – hard and jagged lines, lots of heavy shading – one a continuation of the other. The man is being cut on the arms, the neck, the legs. He's dangling in the blackness, only a tiny square of window light high to his left. Wren and Carlos, Jr. have kitchen knives with serrated edges. First Wren cuts into the man then my son does the same, mimicking her but on the opposite side of the body. They have sliced into the femoral arteries on the thighs, the carotids on the neck. The man is quickly hidden by his own blood. The blood covers him and washes down his hips, chest and head and onto the dirt floor a few inches below him.

Wren is teaching my son.

"I HOPE YOU talk to Dr. Allison about your father."

"That's my business."

"Have I interfered?" Mother is at the kitchen sink washing her coffee cup, the sleeves of the kimono rolled to the elbows. "I'm just saying, that's all. This divorce could be a blessing."

"You can't be serious."

"Have a blessing *aspect*. What's wrong with an aspect? It'll force you to feel other losses, especially about Daddy. You don't think little girls feel hurt? Get angry?"

"We're not having this discussion."

After the Yom Kippur War – this was 1973 or 4 – my father came home and stayed with us for less than a week. Then one afternoon he packed his small brown leather suit case, kissed us goodbye, walked out of our home and left us forever.

That was that.

He gave us no warning, no reason and no letters I know of, no cute photos of himself dressed in tribal hats and robes. Mother had called his friends, the ones she knew, but everybody was as bewildered and as stunned as Mother and I. All of them told us how little this event resembled my father's usual behavior. I also remember several investigators over the years, at least three men and two maybe three women. Mother spent a fortune and some of that money was in her pre "Dr. Betty" days. But they got nothing, zero, my father had disappeared off the planet. Mother said he must have been planning this for awhile and did what he needed to do.

"I've decided to pay for my own therapy," I say. This just comes out of me, nothing angry, nothing defiant.

My mother is still standing at the kitchen sink. She's drying her coffee cup with a red and white striped hand towel and studying me. It feels like she studies me for awhile. Her lips have a little bit of a smile.

"I don't mind, you know."

"I want to tell you my therapy is none of your business and believe it. I can't do that if your paying."

"You like Dr. Allison." It's a statement.

"Today I do."

"Okay. That's good enough for me."

It's not that Daddy simply left us. Men and women abandon their families every day. It's not how he left us, either. There are as many reasons for leaving a family as the people who do it. No, none of that.

It's the *way* he left us.

He left with his reasons unexplained. The getaway became a space waiting for motives and clues. Mother and I are forever filling that emptiness, often in the most destructive ways. We dump whatever fantasies and anxieties we feel on any particular day. And let's be honest, many days it's a potpourri of shit.

TEN

"THIS MICHAEL PERSON, he called your son?" Dr. Allison has stopped writing in her notebook. She watches me but her face shows no particular feeling, not a hint.

"Last night, maybe ten-thirty." Seconds go by and I wait for Dr. Allison to look at me. When she finally does, I can take it for about a second before I have to look down at my lap. It's bizarre. "My son insisted we go get him – Michael, I mean. We had to drive to Nicetown which is near Broad and Eire. So I took Mother's Lexus. Needless to say, she was beyond thrilled. But that's where the boy was hiding. What does she expect my son and I to do, walk? Have you ever been in a subway station at night?"

"You're saying the boy left AMA?"

"...did what?"

"Against the advice of a doctor."

"Yes, he just got up and left," I tell her. "Carlos, Jr. had given him our phone number, put it under his pillow. The boy was sleeping, I guess. You have to understand, my son had a ton of friends before he came here. He happens to be a very social kid, always has been. I've some guilt about the situation, pulling him out of school and so on. Not that he'd stay with his father. If it's between me and Carlos, Sr., it's me every time."

"Wasn't Michael a stranger?"

"He's twelve, a boy."

"But still a stranger."

"Well he's Edward's nephew." I don't get it. Is she asking what's the connection?

"I'm sorry, refresh my memory."

"The guy with the cane." I'm a little annoyed. I've mentioned Edward many times.

Dr. Allison nods and writes in her notebook. My cheeks go hot. Now I feel embarrassed about having an attitude. I hate it when she nods and doesn't say anything.

NICETOWN ISN'T THE crime area it used to be when I was a kid. But it's not downtown Salt Lake City, either. Philly police have been known to guard the Broad and Eire subway station with German Shepherds. These are big dogs with big teeth and they hate everybody but the cops who feed them.

The boy's sitting on a bench at the end of the platform. Shadows and white light cover the concrete floor and the dirty white tile walls. Disinfectant tries to mask a slight urine smell in the damp air. Posters of exotic tan women smoking cigarettes or wearing elaborate sunglasses are on the walls, all the women smiling from behind him. These are the faces of a new America. They are not white, they are not black, they are not any one thing, but they're very pretty.

"Are you Michael?" I say.

"...yes, ma'am." His voice is barely audible.

I'm feeling uneasy. His arms and face are wrapped in white bandages and he has on sunglasses and a red Phillies baseball cap. Michael resembles a younger and chunkier version of Claude Rains in *The Invisible Man*. That was our favorite movie, Mother's and mine – or Mother's. But I liked it, too. We would sit on our brown corduroy sofa with a bowl of popcorn between us and turn out the lights. Mother and I were like children waiting to be scared. But the movie wasn't very frightening, not like a Dracula or a Frankenstein. It's a good one, though. Claude Rains was always more sad than evil.

"Are you in pain, Michael?"

"No, ma'am."

He wears white gloves, too. Every part of him is covered.

"He looks like the guy in that movie," Carlos, Jr. says.

"Let's keep our thoughts to ourselves," I say.

My son and I also watch *The Invisible Man*. Usually we see the movie on Halloween, it's become a family tradition.

"WHAT COMES TO mind about Michael?" Dr. Allison says.

"Well Carlos wanted to know all about him. I did too, I guess. But my boy will ask anybody anything, you know kids. The second we get into the Lexus, my son wants the whole story. But Michael didn't seem bothered by that. He said he expected people to be curious."

I'm hoping Dr. Allison will ask me more questions but she settles into her chair and begins writing in the notebook again. Her forefinger hooks a short strand of gray hair about her ear. Once more I am alone in this beige and leather landscape and she's the audience anticipating my monologue.

"Michael said that after his mother died his father became a very different person, very angry. And he hid Michael in the basement – to live, forced him. Five or six years, the boy said. And he's only how old now, twelve? I mean who knows for sure but that's what Michael told my son and me. His father bought a leather dog collar, along with some steel chain. The collar had a lock on it and the chain let Michael walk around – he could reach the corners, that sort of thing – but he could only get halfway up the steps."

God. I'm not sure I can remember what Michael told my boy and me and I start to feel panicky. It's like when somebody drives up and wants directions to this or that place and my mind goes blank. It's not that I don't know how to get there, I do. But I'm afraid I won't do a good job and I usually tell the person I'm from out of town and maybe the gas station down the road has directions. That's what therapy is like, exactly like that, except there's no gas station.

"...take your time," Dr. Allison says.

She also reads minds.

"The mother died of cervical cancer. Michael said he always reminded his father of her. His face, mostly, the nose and chin."

Grief had overwhelmed his father, that's what the father told him. "I can't bear to look at you, anymore," the father had said. Unbelievable. Who puts a collar on a child and leaves him in a basement? The man's self-involvement is almost comical in its blackness, its hideousness. Oh daddy, poor daddy. He doesn't get that he's torturing his own son. Or listening to Michael, it sounded that way. It sounded like the father was so caught up in himself and his grief, or whatever, that he simply didn't get it. It also seemed as if Michael needed to excuse the man's behavior.

I tell this to Dr. Allison and I can hear the emotion in my voice.

WE ARE PARKED outside Edward's row house, Carlos, Jr., Michael and myself. We are on the opposite side of the street, a decent view. It's eleven-thirty, maybe midnight, I don't know. A living room light is on but the Venetian blinds are shut.

"...I'm sorry," Michael says.

"That's all right."

I had driven us to Mother's townhouse then Michael said he'd changed his mind and wanted to go back to his Uncle Edward's place and I drove us back. It's been that sort of night. We've been sitting in the car for awhile now. I'm not sure what the boy truly wants.

"Are you afraid?" I say him.

"No, ma'am."

"Does this have to do with your bandages, Michael?" It's the first time I've mentioned the bandages. I'm surprised my son hasn't mentioned them, either. We are far more polite than I'd thought. And I say, "Were you burned, did someone do that to you?"

"No, it's a condition."

"You mean like a disease?" Carlos, Jr. says.

"People get it from their families." Michael is in the front of the car on the passenger's side and he's looking across the street at his uncle's house as he talks. "It's, you know, inherited."

The doctor at Little Sister's had told him about his condition and ordered the bandages. No one was sure how his new environment would affect him. But that was all he knew about it.

"Something with your skin?" I say.

"Yes, ma'am. When I'm in the dark my skin gets very dark. It can get as black as the room. I almost disappear then. And when the room becomes lighter my skin gets gray."

"You're like the invisible man." Carlos, Jr. is impressed.

But I don't get it. "Not white?"

"No, ma'am. It's a very light gray."

Maybe that's as bright as a basement gets," Carlos Jr. says.

I'm not sure if that's right but I like my son's way of putting two and two together. "Pretty good, kiddo."

Michael has quit looking out the window. A car passes us, headlights long and yellow. Maybe the boy is looking for his uncle or maybe looking away is how he can discuss this thing. Like the times I cannot look at Dr. Allison. Many times I feel too embarrassed or too uncomfortable, I don't know what it is. Logically there is no reason for it. She's usually kind. Maybe there are times Michael can't look at Carlos, Jr. and me.

I wish I knew him better.

"Only gray or black," I say. "Nothing else?"

"Uncle Edward says my mom had a sister who was pale."

"You mean an albino?"

"He called it pale."

"I'D LIKE TO help Michael," I say. "But I don't know what to do, where to start. I mean you're a doctor. What do you think?"

There's no reply.

"I need you to talk to me," I say. This silence thing is getting very annoying.

"Look I can appreciate your concern." Dr. Allison places the top on her fountain pen. She leans back in her leather chair and holds the ends of the pen between the thumb and forefinger of both hands. "But what you say about Michael is more important than doing something about him. Talking allows us to understand your thoughts, how you're perceiving a situation, how you make sense of things. What isn't appropriate is you and I trying to understand Michael's problem. It might be a worthy use of your time but it's not your therapy. That would be *his* therapy."

"This is too self-centered."

"Hopefully, yes." Dr. Allison is looking at the pen

and smiles to herself. "I will make you a deal. I'll tell you what I know about these skin conditions. Or the little I know about them. But if I do, I'll expect you to understand when I don't respond to your questions."

"That's fine. Explain whatever you can." It's not fine, really. This woman can hurt my feelings in a heartbeat. But I'm overly sensitive and I know it. I need stop taking everything personally.

At least she's honest, I'll give her that.

"Michael's aunt probably is an albino," she says.

Dr. Allison also says it's a genetic condition called achromatosis, a partial or complete absence of skin color. The melanocytes or pigment cells produce a chemical called melanin. It's that chemical that protects the skin from UV rays. But if cells stop producing melanin or produce too much of it, the shift in skin color will become very dramatic.

"These melanocyte dysfunctions can also be passed to other generations," Dr. Allison says. She's thumbing through the pages of her notes. Then she stops and looks up at me. "It can be a son, a daughter. Nephews, nieces. They may not get achromatosis but they may develop different types of melanocyte issues. Also, other things can agitate their conditions, a stressful environment or situation. Of course a family member could get lucky and have a dormant gene and escape the problem altogether."

"When you say a stressful environment, you mean like a basement?"

"For five or six years? Absolutely."

WHAT ABOUT SCHOOL?" I say to Michael. We are still in Mother's Lexus, the boy and me in the front seats, Carlos, Jr. in the back. "Didn't your school send a person – a social worker, a teacher – to see what you were doing, why you weren't going to class?"

The night is clear with many stars and an almost full moon. Michael is still looking out the passenger window at his uncle's row house.

"We moved here after my mom's funeral," he says. "Daddy thought being closer to Uncle Edward would be good for us."

Michael had lived in his father's basement from the age of five or six until a month ago when the man died. He'd been a diabetic with a severely damaged heart. The courts granted the father's older brother, Edward, custody.

"You never registered?" I say, talking about his education.

"Uncle Edward home schools me."

"What about the years with your father? What things did you know?"

"I knew my ABCs, how to read simple words. I knew all that before mom died. We practiced my ABCs every day." Michael turns and looks at my hand on the steering wheel but not my face. I don't want to stare but I do, those bandages, the sunglasses. How can I not stare at that? "Daddy put her things in the basement with me," he says. "Her clothes and things. Her books. She used to read a lot. I wanted to do that, too. And I learned to read her books."

"Hey can we go inside? *Please.*" Carlos, Jr. says this from the backseat. He's patting the headrest like it's a tom-tom. My son can get antsy very quickly and we've been in the car for awhile. "C'mon, Michael," he says. "Let me see your basement."

"It isn't the same one," Michael says.

"You don't have a room?" I'm not sure I heard him right and I start getting nervous immediately. I feel my stomach cramp. I take a breath and try to calm myself. "You should have your own room. Wouldn't you like that? A regular room – with a bed and a desk?"

"I'm used to living in dark places."

DR. ALLISON HAS stopped taking notes and she's watching me again. I think I notice concern or something like that but can't look at her for too long. And when I look at her a second time, there's nothing about her face that shows a feeling.

"I don't believe Michael," I say. "I simply don't. A child needs a cheerful room." Since last night my stomach hasn't stopped cramping. I know my anxiety is about the boy, maybe other things but certainly about him. "Do you believe what he's saying, about how he likes living in dark places?"

Nothing.

Dr. Allison is being true to her word.

"Will you answer, please?"

"What are your thoughts about it?"

"Is that the best you can do?"

God I hate therapy. Well maybe not hate. But I don't get it and I don't like it. Yet here I am, so who's the fool? And I happen to be the individual paying for this now. Oh yes. Starting two sessions ago, *I* began paying, *I'm* the responsible person.

Mother finds all this terribly amusing. I've become the amusing daughter, Dr. Betty's court jester. Let's make fun of the crazy divorcée who slices up her furniture with a kitchen knife and runs in front of a taxi. What a funny little girl. Mother is like a dealer who gave me my first therapy fix for free. Now *I'm* paying and snorting.

"How does it feel being a grown up?" Mother enjoys saying.

So who's the fool?

"Don't miss this opportunity," Dr. Allison says. "You must take advantage of these moments. Tell me your thoughts."

"Are you aware that I'm paying you?" I mean who's in charge here.

"I am. You're improving."

I TELL MICHAEL and Carlos, Jr. to wait in the living room. Edward's house smells of spinach and pot roast. Or some type of beef, I don't know what. I also tell the boys to turn on the TV and watch something. I have taken it upon myself to search the upstairs and the downstairs and see if Edward is home. More than likely he's sleeping. I decide to start with the bedroom first. I could've just as easily started in the basement and worked my way up. Or I could stand in the middle of the living room and call his name.

You-hoo, Edward? Are you there? Olly Olly oxen free. Come out, come out where ever you are.

But why startle the old guy? No, I'll go upstairs and work my way down. I'm the sort of person who likes to do a thorough job – a detail person, a leave no-stone-unturned type.

There is a small study and a bedroom and bath upstairs. The double bed has a red and white striped spread covering it and the top of the spread is neatly tucked about two pillows. A pair of leather slippers are next to the bed, near the nightstand. A clock with green digital numbers reads, 12:38 AM.

No sign of Edward.

I walk down the gray carpeted stairs and go toward the kitchen and an open door between the refrigerator and the stove. Here is something peculiar: I *know* that the open door leads to the basement but I don't know why I know it. I mean why would I know it?

Michael and Carlos, Jr. still sit on the couch in front of the TV. The living room is all shadow except for the white glow of the screen. Gunshots and the rubbery shriek of tires tells me this isn't a movie I'd let Carlos,

Jr. watch, even on my worst day.

I also notice a gun cabinet next to the TV – or rifle cabinet, I don't know what you'd call. Inside the glass and wood case is a shotgun.

"Is that your uncle's," I say to Michael, nodding toward the cabinet.

"My Dad's. *Was* my Dad's. It's a Remington 870." The boy likes telling me the name, I can tell.

"He hunted?"

"Ducks, yeah."

"Did he ever take you with him?"

"I wasn't allowed out."

"Never?" I say. It's difficult to fathom. "I can't believe you've never been outside. You've never been to the mall? To a movie?"

"The sun hurts my skin."

More gunshots on the TV, more cars turning corners way too quickly, Michael goes back to watching the chase with Carlos, Jr. I believe a boy's fascination with cars and firearms are prewired.

But anything to keep them occupied.

The narrow steps leading to the basement are made of unfinished wood, maybe pine. A massive darkness is below the steps. It's broken only by a high tiny window of dim moonlight.

I stop at the bottom of the stairs and wait for my eyes to adjust. How am I supposed to see down here? The ground feels hard and lumpy, more like packed dirt than rock. I don't walk very far before my foot hits something solid and I hear a muffled *uhhh* sound.

It's Edward.

His feet are bound at the ankles. The white rope is long and thrown over a wood beam above us and tied off somewhere in the darkness. His lower body has been lifted slightly. His arms are also tied and there's a cloth about his mouth. He looks up at me with wide frightened eyes, his shoulders and hips wriggle back and forth.

"Is that you?" I say, kneeling beside him.

"...*uhhh*..."

"Try not to exert yourself."

A folded white handkerchief is on the ground near him; and next to the handkerchief, a small amber bottle and a kitchen knife with a serrated edge. I know this is the knife from my kitchen in Chicago and I recognize the bottle of chloroform I bought two days ago. Several feet beyond us and to the right I see my large black canvas bag. This scene is no different than the sketches of Wren I discover on my drawing table. I know these things are mine but that's all I know. And I keep quiet in the darkness. I stay beside Edward.

"...*uhhh*," he says.

And I wonder what I have been up to and what I aim to do.

@*wren&me1* Nothing like an earthquake to let you know who's in charge. Not I. Wren says I'm a wuss. I say: only when the situations pick me.

ELEVEN

"I'M VERY GLAD you called." Sister Kathrin says this as we're walking up the stairs to my studio. "I've been praying for the boy."

"Well that can't hurt."

"I like to think so."

She climbs onto the gray velour chair I have placed next to my drawing board. I forget her tininess. At three-foot-two, Kathrin is the height of a four or five year old but with a middle-aged face. Afternoon sunlight reflects off her wire-rimmed glasses and the white head covering that frames her round face.

"Is Michael here?" she says.

I'm not prepared to answer that one right now. First I want us to talk about him. No, let me re-phrase. I want *her* to talk about him.

I MUST HAVE been ready to do some killing. I think back to the sketches of

Wren and my son hoisting Edward by his bound legs. They had used the same type of clothesline rope I'd used. In the sketches, the two of them bleed Edward. I didn't go that far but I saw my kitchen knife and the amber bottle next to him. I don't remember but I must have used the chloroform before I dragged his skinny butt to the basement.

Did I do that?

I can't deny my things being in Edward's

basement, my black canvas bag, the serrated knife, the amber bottle. I'm guilty, guilty, guilty. My only defense is the same defense I've had from the very beginning, and who'll believe that? The experience of last night is no different than my experience of being a stranger to my own sketches. I know my things like I know my style. But the acts themselves – drawing the sketches, drugging and tying Edward's ankles and arms – these acts are nothing but dark holes.

Maybe Dr. Allison is right. She says there is so much rage in me that I'm fleeing from myself, fleeing from what I feel. She says I'm in a very dangerous place. And not dangerous just for me. Who's going to take care of Carlos, Jr. if I get violent and crazy? Who's going to be his mother and love him as much as I do?

"WHY WOULD A boy want to live in the darkness, a basement?"

I'd like to say, how can Michael *want* to live in a basement with a collar around his neck and chained to the wall? But who can say that out loud? I can't. I don't even like thinking it.

"A person gets used to a particular way of living," Sister Kathrin says. "It's like a criminal who's been in jail for years. Many don't do well on the outside. A man will commit a crime just to go back to the life he knows. Women, too."

Kathrin sips the iced tea I made for her. She's still sitting in the gray velour chair by my drawing board. Her feet are an inch or two off the seat. Her shoes are black with double knotted black laces. I'm on my stool in front of her and occasionally I glance down at the drawing board and the sketches of Wren and my son. These are the ones where they've tied Edward's ankles together.

"You've heard of Stockholm Syndrome?" she says.

"On TV. But I didn't pay attention."

"It's a simple horror." Kathrin is balancing the glass of iced tea on her knees with one hand. Little legs, little hands, little everything. "It's all about the kindly person who locks you in chains. 'Oh I'm sorry, so sorry,' the person says. 'But what can I do?' that sort of thing. Of course he's not kind at all. If it wasn't for him, you wouldn't be in chains. But after awhile, the victim forgets that and just notices the kind words or the occasional favor."

"You mean Michael's father?"

"I mean whoever," Sister Kathrin says. "But, okay, Michael's father. Love becomes the brief lack of abuse."

"What about Edward?"

"The brother. Yes well. We have questions about him, too."

WHEN I FOUND Edward in the basement last night, I'd first cut the gag away from his mouth. He immediately tilted his head to the hard dirt floor and began to cough and dry heave but he couldn't get anything up.

"How did you get into my house?" he'd said. His voice was phlegmy and weak.

"...who are you?"

I didn't answer him, not right away. My immediate thought was to get Michael and my son out of there. I busied myself gathering the kitchen knife, the handkerchief and the amber bottle of chloroform. I was shoving them into my big canvas bag. But I'd nod and look serious as he talked. *I understand your concern*, I said. *What a horrible way to wake up in your own home*. Meantime I'm shoving stuff into my bag. I couldn't get out of that place fast enough.

"You did this to me," Edward said. Very out of it, though. The man talked like someone who didn't know if he was awake or asleep.

"No, no. I saved you."

"How did you get into my house?"

"You invited me," I said.

"I didn't invite shit."

You're not from England. That was my thought.

Here I'm packing for the Great Get-Away. I'm thinking, what proof do I have that Edward's done anything wrong to the boy? Michael likes dark places. If Edward is also keeping him in a basement, couldn't he be weaning him from such an environment, rehabilitating him. Maybe Edward is okay and I'm the crazy person. That wouldn't be a news bulletin. Then somewhere in my weighing the pros and cons, it occurs to me that Edward has an American accent. It's the first time I have actually heard him speak. His talk behind the curtain in Lester's room had always been whispered or muted. And I hadn't heard Michael at all. When I realized Edward was an American and therefore not my father, a depressed feeling had dropped over me.

The man wasn't from England. And if he wasn't from England, where did that leave me? Nowhere. Once again I am nowhere. Not that I really believed the man was my father. But the loss of hope is always more devastating than whatever's true.

"Where were you born?" I said.

"I'll tell the police. I know your face."

"WHAT QUESTIONS?" I say to Sister Kathrin. "You said you had questions about Michael's uncle. Concerns."

"The uncle lived a block from Michael and the father." Kathrin has crossed her legs at the ankles and she's holding the glass of iced tea with both hands. "And Edward was a frequent visitor – at least two or three times a week. The police had interviewed

Michael's neighbors. People said they'd seen a man with a cane enter the house many times."

"You think Edward knew?"

"The brothers were close."

"Was Michael ever hurt?"

That isn't a question I want to ask. Believe me, it isn't. It's like driving down a highway and seeing an accident. Nobody wants to see injured people. But inevitably you slow the car and look at the broken glass and what's at the side of the road. How can anyone not do that? And so I have my questions. Did the two brothers hurt him, did they beat him, was there anything sexual? Questions like these are what comes to mind. Do you collar and chain a boy and that's it? Nothing more? If the father was sick enough to use a collar and chain on his son, why would he stop there? What else did he think about doing, what else did he do?

"He's here with you, isn't he?" Sister Kathrin is studying me, the sunlight on the wire rim of her glasses. "I can keep him safe, you know."

"The father was hurting the boy?"

"We found things. Paraphernalia."

"What things?"

"...things. What's the difference?"

This is no surprise but that doesn't mean I don't feel stunned when I hear it out loud. It's like guessing about a bad truth but guessing right doesn't make it go away and it doesn't bring satisfaction. What sort of father does this to his child? My imagination is already churning up pictures, this and that, the welts and the scars, how the boy's screams are muted.

"I don't think you can keep Michael safe," I say. The sister is a decent person, well intended, a better person than me. But that's not good enough. "I like you, I really do," I tell her. "And the sisters have taken good care of my grandfather. But the boy's different. You couldn't protect the boy the first time."

"We didn't do the best job, I know."

"I'm not looking for a confession."

"...you *do* have him."

"The brothers were close, you said. Michael's uncle visited frequently." I'm looking at one of the sketches of Wren and my son. Considering the tension I'm feeling in my stomach and in the center of my chest, I sound amazingly calm. "Talk about Edward. I want to know about him and the brother."

"He's a responsible guardian. Edward is the one who brought Michael in for treatment. Social services believe he's a good influence."

"And you. What do you believe?"

I THINK I saw Wren in the corner of Edward's basement, her small slim body amid shadows. I'd yet to untie the old man's arms and feet. He still laid on the lumpy dirt floor and he would periodically writhe about, trying to loosen the ropes that held him.

Beyond Edward and toward the far right corner was where I thought I saw Wren or at least her silhouette.

"Get me loose," he said and began more squirming.

"Don't hold your breath."

"I'll call the police. You think I won't?"

"You know I actually thought you were my father," I'd said. "You have a cane. You dress well. There's a certain elegance about you. What do people call it? It's that French thing – *savoir faire*. Isn't that it? You know what *savoir faire* is, what it means? It's knowing what to do, no matter the situation. 'Know how,' that's what it is. That's what my daddy had, that 'know how.' That grace under fire." Or it's what I'd imagined as a child.

"But you aren't that, I don't think."

"Untie me *now*, do it *now*."

In the end, Edward was skinny and pale and rude. A man of little couth. Yes, that was him, exactly. Little couth. He didn't know how to do anything. Except maybe torture boys, he knew how to do that. You can't put all the blame on a child who likes dark places.

"Why is Michael in bandages?" I said.

"I don't have to talk to you."

"Yeah you do. You really do."

"Fuck yourself," Edward said and wriggled and flopped about. He kept saying the same thing over and over, "Fuck yourself. Fuck yourself."

"Why is your nephew in bandages?" I said again.

"Who the hell *are* you?"

"The person who can untie your ass."

That calmed him down. He shut right up. And God that was fine with me. I was getting exhausted just listening to the man. How I could have ever fantasied or hoped that Edward might be my father is incomprehensible. But he wasn't the first or the last. Mother's right, I used to see my father on every street corner.

Dr. Allison uses the word "ambivalent." Having two opposing feelings about the same person, is how she describes it. But it could be anything. You could have opposing feelings about a sandwich or a dress or a movie. "It's how you keep him alive," she has told me. That I don't understand. It's one of those passing things she'll say and I'm too much of a chicken shit to ask, "What the hell are you talking about?"

So note to self: *I'm paying for this, an explanation is due.*

The ambivalence about my father is fairly easy to see. On the one hand I hate him without mercy and take it personally that he wasn't around for me. Who wouldn't want to be around cute adorable me? Lovely blond curls, a little space between my front teeth. Seriously. It makes you feel bad about yourself, unlovable. But this bastard was either stupid or blind. On the other hand, I love him for how he could have loved me if he'd wanted to. That's the real heart stopper. You imagine how love could have been. Dr. Allison is always preaching that one. In therapy you get the intellectual part first. Only later will the past greet you as a feeling, something emotional, relatable. It's the intellect and the feeling *together* that has the magic.

"I've seen you," Edward was saying; still threatening me. "I can identify you. I can say, 'Yes, that's her. That's the one who broke into my home. That's the one who drugged me and pushed me down the basement stairs. Look at my bruises. Look at these cuts. Who would do that to an old man? What sort of person?' And don't think I won't do that, *deary*. Don't you think it for a minute."

"Did you just call me 'deary?' Who calls anybody that?"

It's true. Even though Americans use the word, it's the English who do it best. Years ago – the 70s, early 80s I'm thinking – there was an English comedy craze in this country. Terry Thomas, Peter Sellers, Margret Rutherford, Kenneth Corner, it's a very big list – Hermione Gingold, for godsake – and all of them, one time or another, used the word "deary." Besides *The Invisible Man*, Mother and I also loved English comedies. We felt our best together when we were sitting on the couch, watching movies on TV.

"...deary deary deary," Edward kept saying.

"God you're an annoying old man."

"Better untie me, *deary*."

Wren was waving to me now, arms above her head,

that corner of the room not so dark anymore. She sat on a neatly made cot, its green Army blanket tucked squarely and firm about the corners, Her skinny legs were crossed, hightops laced half the length of the shoe, and her presence had the on again-off again clarity of a dream. She would appear if I didn't stare too closely. She was there if I used the corners of my eyes. But what was gathered next to her got me more unnerved than seeing her. What I saw was a collar and a bunched pile of chain. A line of that chain lead away from its pile and into the shadows of the ceiling.

"They'll lock you up," Edward said. Meaning the cops, I guessed.

"I don't think so."

I was already walking toward the cot. As I got closer, Wren became vague then part of the shadows and I could not see her. But the collar and the chain remained. I had turned to Edward, holding them – the leather collar in one hand, a length of the chain in the other – and I saw the color and the anger leave his face.

"Will you be explaining this?" I'd said.

TWELVE

"EVERYTHING HAPPENED VERY fast."

"So you have no plan?" Dr. Allison says to me.

"Sometimes people act first."

"That's like your therapy." Today she's letting nothing slide. But her voice has no particular emotion. It's more matter-of-fact. "As long as you keep doing your therapy out there—" her hand holding the fountain pen gestures hitchhiker style to the white wall behind her chair "—we can't do it in *here*."

"I couldn't just leave Michael."

Dr. Allison is writing in her notebook and doesn't answer me. Or won't. She's dressed casual this afternoon, pressed khakis and a white t-shirt under a light gray cotton pullover. Totally collected, almost other worldly. I bet anything that the air conditioner is set at a perfect 72 degrees.

"Would *you* have left him?" Now I'm annoyed.

"Why not say what comes to mind."

"That's your answer for everything."

"Isn't it your therapy?"

See. She fucks you with logic. Excuse my French. But there's no way else to describe it and no way to have a decent argument with her. And today I'd like one of those pots and pans arguments, some yelling, some throwing, some crazy. Who the hell knows why, I don't know why. No, that's not true. I knew I'd get questioned today for bringing Michael home with me.

121

My son's absolutely thrilled with the idea, of course. My mother is compliant with it but bewildered. And me, I think I did the right thing but I'm ambivalent. I know that by taking Michael home I've just jumped knee deep into shit. It's hard fooling myself, anymore.

"YOU WANT TO go back to the sisters?"

This wasn't a threat, I didn't know what Michael wanted. I know little about him and nothing about twelve year olds. And I'll probably know nothing about twelve year olds until my son reaches that age and he and I go through it together. Maybe that's not completely true. I do have the feeling that Michael and I are both learning about what it is we need and want from the world.

"Here's fine," Michael said. The boy sat on the inflatable mattress I'd set up for him next to Carlos, Jr.'s bed. And what an odd sight. He had on his sunglasses and his white gloves and he also wore a sleeveless undershirt and boxers, his arms and legs still wrapped in white gauze. "I like the sisters but I don't like that place," he says. "People can come in and talk to you whenever they want. People the sisters think are okay but people you don't want to talk to."

"You mean your uncle."

"Anybody. But him, too."

We'd just left his uncle's, Michael, me and Carlos, Jr. We were now at Mother's house and it was very late. Carlos had already fallen asleep, a skinny tanned arm draped off the side of the bed. Michael and I were talking in whispers.

"Do you need any sort of treatment?" I said. "Anything I should know about?"

"I have an ointment."

This was when he took off his gloves and unwound the bandage up to his right elbow. His hands and his beefy arm were a pale gray color. But the medication was for others things. Old scars and newer ones went the length of the arm. Some of the newer ones were not quite healed.

"I'M GOING TO turn on my recorder," Dr. Allison says. The recorder is on the small wood table next to her chair. It's a silver or metal device no bigger than the palm of her hand.

"...why do that?" I'm confused, immediately anxious.

"This is serious business." She's been listening and writing her notes for half the session but in the last five minutes my talk about Michael has made her stop and look at me. "Serious for the boy, yes. There's no question. But for you, too. Different but very serious in its own way. People can't go around stealing other people's children."

"I couldn't leave him."

"Understood. But do you see the problem?" The palms of her hands are perched on her knees and she has the look of a vigilant bird. "Here's what you've done – instead of reporting Edward, you've kidnapped his nephew."

"But the boy has new wounds," I say. "Some of them look infected. I mean I don't think Michael uses his ointment. You know how children are, they don't bother with these things. And it's obvious Edward neglects him." Why doesn't she get that? Many times I simply don't understand Dr. Allison's point of view. "I'm guessing the uncle is beating him. But if he is – beating the boy, I mean – why would he also take Michael to Little Sisters?"

"Why Edward does something shouldn't be your concern right now." Dr. Allison has placed her notebook and pen on the small table next to the recorder. "You should be directing Michael to the people who can help him. Whether it's Social services or Little Sisters, whoever. And let me be very clear, if you don't report this, I'll have to do it. I'm bound to do it, I have no option."

"I intended to call Sister Kathrin."

"When? When will you do that?"

"...I don't know. After my therapy."

"Here, let me see you do it," Dr. Allison says and hands me her cell.

LAST NIGHT'S TALK with Michael left me feeling terrified for him. I easily imagined myself in Edward's basement, in that darkness. I'd imagined being alone the way he had been alone. No one there to rescue me, no one to scoop me up and take me away. My empathy felt sprawled and sticky like wet pie dough; I couldn't get myself detached from it. It clung to me, the bottoms of my feet, my hands webbed in it. I had listened to him and I had panicked. It was too personal.

"You must have been scared," I said. We were sitting on the inflatable mattress

I'd put next to Carlos, Jr.'s bed. "What did you think, living like that? How did you feel?"

"I don't remember, probably afraid at first." Michael was letting me put some of the ointment on his skin. It had a fishy smell and I tried being gentle but once in awhile he'd wince. Then he said, "But it was the place where I lived – the basement – it was, you know, my home."

The bedroom had moonlight on the wood floor and across Carlos, Jr.'s white top sheet. Carlos was asleep and I could hear him breathing steadily and quietly behind us.

"How did your father treat you?" I said. I wasn't sure how to talk about his scars; whether I wanted to talk about them. But there are things that draw me in whether I want them to or not.

"Daddy treated me good."

We were both whispering so we wouldn't wake my son.

"What about your uncle?"

"He treats me good, too."

"All the time?"

"Most times."

"I NEVER ACTUALLY thought Edward was my father," I say.

"...never?" Dr. Allison is still watching me.

It's always Truth Time with her. You can't just say something. Heaven forbid I should chit-chat – you know, the way people do? How's that golf swing? Still playing the piano? Pleasantries, that sort of thing. Around her, I can't arc an eyebrow the wrong way.

Never? Dr. Allison has that tone. Like, "Are you sure you want to go with that answer?"

I cannot speak for little boys but little girls who grow up without daddies look for them everywhere. And they don't stop looking. Ever. Okay, happy? The very popular Dr. Betty – who also admits to being my mother – has told me the exact same thing on many occasions. So yes I do have that Hope Thingie in the back of my mind. *Maybe this one is my father*, that thought is there if the man is old enough and has those features I've always imagined my father to have, that well turned out look, slim, nice suit, an English accent, movie star eyes. And of course a cane, always the cane.

"He didn't have an English accent," I say.

"And what if he'd had one?"

"The accent? I don't know." I'd have to think about it. "I suppose Edward would continue on my list of possibilities."

Dr. Allison has begun writing in her notebook again, and I'm glancing about the office. There's a stoic elegance to it, very tidy. Everything is earth tinted and gray. But there's an emptiness in it, too. I feel that more than see it.

"The accent doesn't make a bit of difference." The woman brushes something from the knee of her khaki pants, lint or something, and she says, "He could be English, he could be Russian, it wouldn't matter. You'd intellectualize all sorts of reasons about how he lost his accent. Or how he never *had* one. This isn't about an accent. This is about avoiding your grief. You avoid grieving the loss of your husband by obsessing about your father. And you avoid grieving the loss of your father by believing you'll discover him just around the corner."

"There's nothing wrong with hope."

"Oh really?" Dr. Allison doesn't believe me for a minute. "Let me tell you something. And you can accept it or not. Hope is what keeps you from your life."

"Pardon me? Hope is a positive thing."

"If it's not being used to hide the truth, yes."

"And what truth is that?" I hear my own indignation.

"That your father is gone forever."

"HOW CLOSE WERE they?" I'd said to him. We were in Carlos, Jr.'s bedroom. Moonlight was coming through the partially open window and turning some of the floor into a narrow silver path. I wanted to know more about Michael's father and his uncle. "You told me your father had come to Philly to be near his brother? Edward is his older brother, didn't you say that?"

"He's a lot older."

"How old are we talking?"

"A lot older, maybe ten years. Maybe it's closer to fifteen. I'm not good with that. But older. My grandfather died a long time ago. Edward was like my father's daddy. Or that's what my father always said."

"So you saw Edward once a week, more?"

"Twice a week, maybe. They'd visit me."

"You mean the basement?"

The three of them would drink and watch movies, mostly. Michael said he liked the cold white wine better than the red. But the red wasn't too bad. He said he liked the way he'd felt after drinking it. There were movies, too. When I asked him what sort of movies, he looked at the moonlight crossing the wood floor and shrugged.

"You know, movies."

"...naked pictures?"

"Just movies."

"Boys like you?" I said.

"Sometimes."

"YOU'RE TELLING ME I should for*get* my father?"

My stomach has become flippy. I feel everything in my stomach. Mother says she's the same way. It's genetic or something, it's what we do. I was becoming anxious just thinking about how it might feel if all my thoughts of J.D. Waye vanished. It would be like he never existed. It would be worse than death. At least a person's death let's the living keep memories. J.D.'s nonexistence leaves me with nothing.

"No, the opposite," Dr. Allison says. "I'm telling you to postpone these hunts for your father and simply talk about him. And do that here with me, that's what I'm saying. When you go on these hunts, you're acting out old memories. You've slipped back into your past, your history. And you don't even know it."

"God it's always the past. That's all you therapists talk about – The Past, like it was a sacred thing. My mother does that, too."

"Because it's where you're living."

"I'm living in Philadelphia."

"Your body's living in Philadelphia. The rest of you is five years old and stuck in old feelings."

I'm looking about Dr. Allison's office again. I think I do that when I get nervous and want to get away from the therapy. There's a peacefulness in it's uncluttered space, very different than what goes on in this room. A person can only take so much crap. I start to feel like I'm being picked apart. It's like a constant assault that blows little holes in you.

"I'm not ready to give him up," I say.

"But this is what it means for you. Don't you see? To talk about your father is to give him up. To quit your search. But you refuse to think it through. How can you give up a person who was never there?"

THIRTEEN

Darling Betty,

I am sitting beside my tent and looking at the clear desert sky and thinking about us. Of course I do that every night. I like us and who we are now and how we are with each other. The two of us, you and I, what can be better than that? Nothing, that's what I think, absolutely nothing better. We have such fun, don't we? Right from the first coffee in our little café on Oldham Street. (Even that hideous guitar player seemed wonderful!) I do miss Manchester.

Tonight I see your face, the way you watch me, the way your eyes gather me in, those lovely kind eyes. I saw that look the first time we met and every day after that. We don't really need anyone else, do we? What a selfish man I am to want to keep you for myself...

I AM READING through my father's letters. The boys and Edward are on my mind, particularly Edward. Mother keeps my father's letters in a Nine West shoe box and the box is now out of Carlos, Jr.'s bedroom and on my drawing board. Afternoon sunlight comes through the skylight and reflects off the white walls and the polyurethane wood floor. I've been going through one letter after the other and I am not sure why I'm doing this – these letters go from embarrassingly B movie romantic to the tediousness of the everyday – but I want clues, I want a hint. As Dr. Allison might say, I'm still on my so called hunt.

Some clue. Anything.

Dr. Betty and her faithful sidekick Carlos, Jr. have gone shopping for black suede pumps. Mother is attending a broadcasters' dinner next week at the Crowne Plaza Hotel in Center City to receive a lifetime achievement award. The reigning queen of Help Me Radio. Dr. Betty believes a lifetime achievement award is the kiss of death. "My career isn't over," she says. "What's wrong with those people?" And Mother is determined to show them that she is not dead yet. Carlos, Jr. thinks he can get another video game out of the deal.

...you know I do, darling Betty. I want you all to myself. We know how to have fun, don't we? I love our routines. Friday nights at the movies, me paying for tickets, you paying for the popcorn and the drinks. There is comfort in each of us knowing what to do. I get enough surprises in my work, it's good that our lives are predictable and without drama. Keep our home time dramas on the silver screen, I say.

I love our Wednesday night dinners out, too. Our favorite restaurant, our favorite table, the waiters know us by name – what could be more satisfying than a waiter coming up to us and saying, "Good evening Mr. and Mrs. Waye, the usual tonight? I love waiters knowing what we like, what pleases us.

But we are also not above moments of spontaneity. Nothing prevents us from saying, "Let's take a trip to New York this weekend. We can see that show we've been wanting to see. Oh and dinner at the Essex House, we love the Essex House." There is much to be said for how you and I live our lives.

Who would change a thing? Not I...

THERE'S NOTHING GRAPHIC about J.D. Waye's

letters, no real violence, no real sex. Well some. But it's a sort of cotton candy violence and sex, a one lick and it's gone thing. He liked writing about danger, how this journalist or than one either got wounded or almost got wounded. There's also lots about how J.D. escaped the many Arabs who wanted his destruction. Or that was what he'd like us to think. They plotted against him, continually. Arabs in tanks. Arabs with knives and guns. Arabs who'd whisper at night outside his tent. Arabs who spoke a secret language and never shaved. These tales sounded like pulp from the thirties and forties. My father was a storyteller, my mother his number one fan. And he *did* like drama – provided it was about him. After reading several of his letters, I get the feeling he hated competition, especially if it stole Mother's attention.

What I notice about this letter I'm reading is *how* my father wanted to see himself and have others see him. He wanted to be seen as a risk taker, a hero, something from the comics or from one of my novels. But this wasn't him, it was so obvious. His job had risks, yes – perhaps even a bullet to the leg, though who knows – but I suspect his stories were puffed and glamorized and not him at all. J.D. Waye liked his home life quiet and he liked his routines. Most importantly, my father wanted to be with Mother and only her. That was his idea of a good life. And perhaps it was.

...I've never understood these party types, these couples who go on vacations with friends. "Let's invite George and Sally. And while we're at it, how about Patrick and Clare? Clare is such a hoot. Love her impersonations." Well good for Clare. Let her hoot with some other couple. God how tedious. Do you remember the time you lost your passport in

Florence? Can you imagine what would have happened if other couples been with us? Talk about a nightmare! Then we would've had to worry about them and their needs and what to do to make THEM feel comfortable. We'd have felt guilt that we might ruin everybody else's vacation. I run scenarios about things like that constantly. But what did you and I do? We made it into an adventure. We got to see the embassy. We met others who'd lost their passports. I loved that part of our vacation! And so did you. "What's the worst that could happen?" we'd said to each other. "Maybe spend another day in Florence? Maybe Two? One of the most beautiful and interesting cities in the world? Oh poor us. Do you think we'll survive?" Ha! This is what I mean. This is how you and I approach the world, how you and I have fun. Do we really need crazy Clare doing another impersonation of Lady Bird? A resounding NO, I say...

I AM IMAGINING Wren sitting in the far corner of my studio. I see her when I glance over the top of my father's letter. She's sitting on the polished wood floor, arm wrapped about her upper legs, chin resting on her knees.

"Some things you shouldn't read," I imagine her saying.

Why those words, why not a positive comment? "I'm pleased you're getting to know your dad." Or, "Not such a bad guy, is he?" Why give her such creepy thoughts? What's wrong with me? After all, I'm the person who invented her, I decide what Wren thinks, what she wears – her black leather coat, her skinny jeans, the earrings – I decide how she acts. Me. If the girl smiles or frowns, it's me drawing whatever expression appears, my pen, my ink, me giving her the words.

"You never used to be this way," she says.

Some truth to that, I think.

Then Wren says, "I used to shock you so easily. 'Where did that come from?' you'd want to know. Like I was the one making it up, saying the words. Like you had nothing to do with it." Her accent is in full British mode, how I picture Daddy talking. She's looking down at her black hightops with the white tips. "You're very different, you've changed, Rhea. But I can't put my finger on why, exactly. No, I take it back.

I *can* put my finger on it. You know we're the same."

"That's not a secret."

"But we pretended it was, didn't we?"

Yes, we did that. I was the one who played it safe and Wren was the one who took the chances. I played the good one and she played my temptation. She was the devil in my wasteland. She offered a voice to darker thoughts, I've always known that. It's an obvious truth, if I'm honest with myself. But maybe I know it better now. Can there be such a thing? To know what you've known but to know it better, to raise the focus of it? This isn't an epiphany. It's a yawn, a slow awaking. No *ah-ha!* moment. It's an "oh-of-course-I-*know*-that" moment – to realize what I do and what I imagine, or realize it some of the time. That's what therapists like Dr. Allison don't tell you. You don't become a new person. This isn't a makeover, or whatever. I'm the same person but I see and feel more of me.

"Some things you shouldn't read," Wren says again.

The afternoon sunlight has become brighter. Perhaps a cloud I hadn't noticed has come and gone. Light reflects between the gloss of the walls and the polyurethane floor and I cannot see Wren clearly. Details are lost. There's the shine of her metal earrings, the tips of her hightops.

"Mother left the letters for us," I say. "For Carlos, Jr. and me."

"Since when do you trust *her*?"

"That's not your business." Listen to that. She has *no* business. It's so easy for Wren to become something other than my invention.

I do have suspicious feelings. But Wren can't tell me anything I do not already know. Dr. Allison once said that to me. *It's a conversation with yourself, between the thoughts and feelings you accept and the ones you don't.* Or something like that, I don't recall the words exactly.

Here's what I suspect. I believe my son was my mother's delivery boy. I believe that's why she didn't think twice about Carlos looking at her letters. I'm the one who's supposed to read them. I'm also the one who would've told her I wasn't interested if she had offered. I don't trust my own mother. Wren is right. Excuse me, *I'm* right. Mother doesn't merely offer me help. She plots help, she schemes. Oh it's well-intended, done out of love, no doubt, but the woman is a bull in a psychic China shop. *Bam, bing! Here take this, go on. It'll help. Bang, bam!* That's her, that's precisely her. That's my Dr. Betty, Queen of Help Me radio.

And why are the letters a big deal? Everything between my parents seems so G rated. That "I dream of holding you" crap. Mother says she used to send Daddy letters sprinkled with her perfume and Daddy would go on and on about how "intoxicated" he'd get "breathing in" her words. God. Corny to their cores, those two, it's enough to make a person cringe.

...the words of an only child, darling, that's how it

was – me, my parents and Lilly the cocker spaniel. You were an only child, too, if memory serves. And let's face it, who doesn't like that? All the toys were mine. Didn't you like having all the toys? I bet you did. Nobody likes sharing their toys, that's why parents have to teach us to do it. But for a time I was the prince and the world was mine. And how often I've imagined you as the beautiful princess with a kingdom of your own, with loved ones who adored you and only you. I can picture you smiling at this, perhaps even a laugh. Wasn't it grand? I think so.

Grander still, we actually found one another. The prince and his princess, the princess and her prince, we are very lucky you and I. We know benevolence, we know worship. We know how to treat the other better and wiser than anyone else. Where many bring candy, flowers and trinkets to bind their love, we simply listen to each other, our eyes fixed, our expressions appropriate to the tale, sad, joyous, perplexed – you name it – we offered the gift of being heard, of being understood and appreciated. We remembered the cooing and ahhh of our parents, the value of it, the excitement. How wonderful I am! we thought. How extraordinary my talents, my ways, my very being! That's what we gave each other, that's what we give today.

We know the symmetry of the two. What is more balanced? What is more perfect? Yin and yang. Life and death. Day and Night. Hot and cold. Odd and even. Active and passive. On and on it goes, this symmetry, this perfection that is the two...

I THINK WREN passed behind me. I feel a warm drift of air on my neck and I can smell – what is it, that smell? – gardenia, maybe. Though a breeze through the open studio window could have just as easily brought the scent. Mother's flower garden, I'm guessing. I look up from reading the letter and I am alone. The breeze causes a sheet of paper to billow and settle on my drawing table.

It's a quickly done pencil sketch of our brick row house on the corner of Elfreth's Alley. Another picture I don't remember doing, but it's obviously mine. Wood shutters, dormer windows, narrow cobblestone street, everything's there. And another something. A man is standing beneath my window, or maybe it's Carlos, Jr.'s room. Yes, my son's room. I recognize the man right away and the drawing so catches me that I let out a tiny shock of air, a *wooo* sound. He looks especially tall and thin in this drawing, as if he'd been stretched to twice his height. The man's like a long evening shadow. His suitcoat is buttoned, his shirt and tie impeccable. There's a folded handkerchief sticking out from the pocket next to his lapel. And he has a cane of course. Both hands are propped on the curved handle of his cane.

I start to feel light headed and I place the sketch face down on the drawing board and take a couple of slow breaths, refocusing on J.D.'s letter. The fast beat of my heart won't quit pushing at the sides of my neck.

...your last letter more than a surprise. I suppose I've been avoiding it. Hurting you isn't what I ever want to do. But I cannot join you in your happiness. I realize what I'm about to say will change us forever, I know that. And I'm sorry, truly sorry. Surely you know how much I adore you. There should be no question in your mind about that. But I cannot celebrate your pregnancy – "our" pregnancy, as you call it (though it is "our" pregnancy only up to the moment of "your" pain) – and I cannot be the husband and the father you have in your mind. To celebrate

this news would be to celebrate the loss of what we have together. How can I do that? Yes, I understand my responsibility. What is it that people say? "You pay to play." I know that's the wrong expression for us. To suggest I thought our life together was a game could not be further from the truth. I take our life together seriously. This is why I could not bear a change in it. And it's why I cannot go on with it. I'll certainly give you whatever monetary assistance you or the court decides, I won't argue that sort of thing. Didn't you know my thoughts on this? Didn't we discuss what we wanted, what we required? I believe we discussed our likes and dislikes right from the beginning. As I recall, these talks began with our first coffee at the café on Oldham Street. Granted it was indirectly stated. It wasn't, "Well if we start to date and fall in love and get married, I don't want babies." It wasn't that. At first, I'm thinking, it was more abstract, wasn't it? More like, "Relationships are complicated enough without adding pets and babies." That sort of thing, we joked about it. Don't you remember? But there were many talks through the months and years. Positions were stated very clearly. And most of the time you seemed to agree with me, didn't you? At least you agreed at the start, the beginning years. Even later on, you didn't disagree. You stayed quiet, basically. That's different than stating your case. Perhaps I ought to have been more sensitive to your silence. But I still say my thoughts on this matter were never a secret. You can't accuse me of being a withdrawn husband, sitting in the corner of the room, hiding behind his newspaper. I was always very good to you and very vocal about my opinions. Oh I can hear you now. "But we were children then," you're saying. "People grow up, J.D. Our lives change. What would happen if everyone thought like you?" But not everyone does think like me, Darling Betty. Nobody thinks like everybody else. That's an argument given by first grade teachers and pastors.

If you change your mind, I pray you will let me know. Abortion isn't the nastiest idea in the world – not in all cases, anyway. The nastiest ideas are the rules we make up for ourselves.

With all my love,
J.D.

FOURTEEN

I HAD INVITED Sister Kathrin over to discuss Michael. A late morning rain patted the living room windows. It was one of those rains where the sunlight kept appearing and disappearing.

"His uncle brought him to us," she said, talking about Edward and the boy. I still felt uncomfortable with her tininess, it was like being with elves or fairies. She and I sat on Mother's green and yellow floral sofa. "When you called yesterday, I thought I'd told you that." She had; I just found it difficult to believe. Then Sister Kathrin said, "Edward was very worried about his nephew. The boy has a history of cutting on himself."

"On him*self*? You get that from the uncle?"

"His medical records," she said. "Michael's a Borderline Personality Disorder. It's a less common diagnosis for boys than it is for girls – statistically, you know. But if you consider his history of mental and physical abuse, it's not out of the question. He's been self-mutilating for years."

"The boy's been living in that hideous basement. He told my son and me he liked 'darker places' – that's how he put it – but I'm not convinced. And I *did* see a dog collar and chain on his cot."

"After your call yesterday, we sent social services out to the house. There was a cot, apparently. But no collar, no chain."

"I swear I saw those things," I said.

"Uh-huh. What were you doing there?"

IT'S EVENING AND Michael and Carlos, Jr. are finally asleep and I am in Dr. Betty's bedroom and thinking about this morning with Sister Kathrin. Mother's plotting her outfit for the broadcasters' dinner next week at the Crowne Plaza Hotel. It's coming down to the Little Black Dress and whatever else, what jewelry, what purse, etcetera and which Little Black Dress works best with her new black pumps. Mother actually knows what goes with what, I'll give her that. The queen of Help Me radio knows her fashion. Now myself, I barely get my jeans on in the morning.

"Where *are* you, Rhea?" It's a typical Mother question, more a comment on my preoccupations.

"With you."

"No you're not. Physically, maybe. But where's the rest of you?"

"It's fine, Mother. I'm here."

"Right. Let me know when you land."

I have too much on my mind. There's this morning's talk with Sister Kathrin, the sketch of Edward looking up at my son's bedroom window – something I obviously drew and promptly forgot, how many times have I done that? – and J.D.'s letter, let's not forget the letter. God what a self-centered A-hole. I'm cluttered with all of it.

"Daddy was quite the shit," I said. The words tumbled out.

"Good. You read the letter."

Mother is looking at herself in the full length mirror. It's attached to the back of the bedroom door. She turns first to the right then the left. A back and forth, back and forth thing. On each turn she's studies her butt while the palm of her hand tries to smooth away the curve of her stomach.

"Why didn't you simply *tell* me?" I said. "Or give me the letter."

"Would you have read it?"

"Probably not."

"You wouldn't have believed me, either."

All right, that's true. It's not that I think my mother's an awful person. She's not; I'll be the first to admit it. But the woman carries extreme baggage – well both of us do, emotional stuff, disappointments or whatever – and it's not easy for either of us to clear a path and talk sense to one another. This isn't either bad or good, okay? It's the way it is. We both know it, I think.

"So no actual trips to the zoo?" I say.

"I wanted you to have something."

"But you made up my life."

"You work with what you got."

"That's the best you can do?" I can't believe her. "That's it? 'You work with what you got,' that's all you have to say? *Moth*er. I do that with Wren, for godsake. I give *her* a history, I give her memories. Basically you're telling me my memories are a fiction, something *you* created."

"Don't overreact, dear."

"*Par*don me? *Par*don me? Hey I'm a fiction. You made me up and I believed you. Don't dismiss this, Mother. Our memories are who and what we are. Isn't that what you say? You therapy types?" I feel my face going hot. I can't find enough air to breathe. "Why exactly am I standing here trying to educate a psychologist? Don't they have any sorts of tests for you people?"

"'You people?' That's what I am to you?"

"A what-you-call-it, a Blind Leading the Blind test?"

"Calm down, Rhea. Most of your memories are true."

"Well lucky me – *la-de-da* – most of who I am is legitimate. How *wonder*ful for Yours Truly. What a blessed person I am. Oh thank you, thank you, Mother. This is just so bizarre, there's not a word for it. Most of me is true. You can't make it up. And how much is that, Mother, the part that's true? Twenty percent? Forty percent? Can I get a ballpark figure here? Oh and do you mind if I use that on my bio? The queen of Help Me radio – my own mother – says *most* of me is true." Could she be anymore of a twit? Seriously. "That's *not* good enough, okay?"

"This isn't fair," Mother says. She has turned from the mirror and her obsession with the Little Black Dress and it's accessories. "I'm getting very tired of being your punching bag, Rhea. Let me tell *you* something, okay? I wish your father hadn't been such a chicken shit. I wish he'd had the balls God gave him and stayed around. Maybe he could take a few punches, occasionally."

"What I got is a phony-baloney history," I say. I'm not chucking this argument, not for a second. "I'm no better than Wren." I stopped and took a couple of breaths and tried to calm myself down. "Let me get this straight. All the memories I have about my father– I mean they aren't that many, really – but all these memories of him reading me bedtime stories, us going to the zoo together, our chats about his war experiences, etcetera – all of that's crap.

"What can I say? I'm not creative in that way."

"What way are we discussing?"

"The way you're creative, dear."

"This includes the desert stuff and the birds?"

"Well he did spend time in the desert."

"Great. Egypt or Palm Springs?"

142

"I did the best I could, Rhea."

"YOU THINK HE'S cutting on himself?" I'd said to the sister. We were still in the living room. "I've heard of Borderline Personalities but this isn't just Michael hurting Michael."

"The father was also abusive to the boy, no question."

"Glad to hear you say that."

"Oh it's not the boy alone."

"If it was *ever* the boy," I'd said.

"You don't think much of the uncle."

"Nothing good, no."

I have an image of Edward cutting on Carlos, Jr. This is why I believe I drew that picture, the one where he's looking up at my son's bedroom window. Dr. Allison would call it an "anxiety picture." It's me drawing what gets me anxious and then disowning it, that's what she thinks. But no doubt Edward's pissed about me taking his nephew. I'm also positive he's a man who plays You Do This to Me and I'll do That to You, a tit for tat mindset. I don't have to dig very far to get that one.

"It's an illness, Rhea. The boy has an illness." Sister Kathrin had placed her hand on top of mine. It was the size of a child's hand, not a middle-aged woman. Her nails were bitten and the knuckles were very rough and pink. Sister Kathrin must scrub them on the hour. She was saying, "And yes, you're right. It does comes from a terrible situation. You can't expect anyone to go through what Michael went through – day after day, many years – and not have it effect him."

"It's the uncle and the father." My stubbornness was emphatically there.

"I'm not defending the father, believe me. He was a man with his own demons." Sister Kathrin was cleaning the lenses of her wire-rimmed glasses with the loose sleeve of her habit. She held the glasses up to the living room window, inspected them then hooked the wire rim about her ears. "We found the evidence," she said. "Or Edward found it, I didn't. And he reported it to the police."

"Edward reported what?"

"You're suspicious."

"What did he find?" I said.

"Movies, other dreadful who-knows-what-to-call it – paraphernalia. Whips and things, things to put over the mouth. Surgical knives, too."

"Michael mentioned movies."

"That's interesting," Sister Kathrin said. "I got nothing from him. He's a very secretive boy, generally."

"Carlos showed him one of my books. I think he likes Wren."

"He needs friends, I've been praying on this."

"He wanted to stay with the uncle," I'd said. "Can you imagine? What kid would do that? Go back, I mean. God I wouldn't. What do you think of Edward?"

"...very smart, very clever."

"So you don't trust him, either."

"I didn't say that."

"THIS IS MY fault," Mother says. She's going through necklaces and bracelets in the dark leather jewelry box on her vanity table. "I should have been honest. What can I tell you? I was young then."

"But you *never* told me." We are still talking about my father the shit.

"You know how it is, Rhea. By the time I got old enough to know better I was also old enough to know how hurt you'd be."

"Okay, okay. Look let's just forget it and go on."

"You give up too easy," she says.

"*Mothe*r. What do you want me to do?"

"Fight for yourself."

"I don't know what that means."

It's still raining out side. I can hear it batting at the windows and the dormers. The lights in the night are runny like watercolors. One of the windows is pulled up a little and I can feel the damp air on my arms.

"I fought for myself when Carlos, Sr. left."

"Getting crazy isn't fighting for anything."

"It sure scared you guys."

"Like I said, Rhea, fight for yourself."

I enjoy my mother being wrong far more than I enjoy her being right. I want to be angry with her – for her lies, for her self-centeredness -- but then I see how she cares about me and how fucking logical she can be – how wise, if you must know – God I hate even saying that – and I want to cry. I want to hold her and I want to cry. I want to thank her for doing the best she could do. I hate it when she's right. I hate it, hate it, and I don't know why. I hate it on principle. I hate it because it's Tuesday evening. But she is right and she's right much of the time. My mother, my queen of Help Me radio. You work with what you got.

"TRUSTING EDWARD IS like trusting the father," I told Sister Kathrin. "These brothers were more alike than different, that's what I think. There *was* a collar. I don't care what Edward says or what social services saw or didn't see. I didn't imagine these things. And there was also a chain, I'm absolutely sure."

"I want to be honest with you." Sister Kathrin said. Her face was framed by her white head covering and she'd been looking out the window at the rainy afternoon. "It hurts my heart to agree – about the brothers. I don't like speaking bad about anybody. We can't know what's in another person's heart. But I think

145

the man got scared, the uncle. I think he did something he shouldn't have and panicked."

"Edward was doing what the father had done."

"...yes. Perhaps."

"I'm thinking that, too," I said.

I felt relieved that Sister Kathrin and I had the same opinion about the uncle. I didn't want to be in this alone. A few days ago I actually had fantasies that Edward might be my father. I knew he wasn't but that didn't stop the fantasies, my wishes to set the world right. And a right and good world for me is always a mother and a father and their child.

"Can't we call somebody?" That was what I'd asked the sister. I didn't think I could protect Michael. Occasionally I have real doubts about protecting my own child.

I never thought about such things when Carlos, Sr. was around. "We could call social services. Get the boy placed with foster parents. I'd even take him, at least temporarily. I'm sure my mother would be fussy but she'd get over it. Or maybe she wouldn't be fussy at all. She's always surprising me."

"There's no proof," Sister Kathrin said. "And the court won't accept our feelings about this sort of thing."

"I *saw* the proof."

"I know, dear."

"But you're not taking what I saw seriously."

"I believe you, Rhea. We wouldn't be having this conversation if I didn't. We have to save this boy and I don't know how to do it. I've never felt more helpless. So you and I have a lot in common in that department. This Edward, I think we're dealing with a man who knows how to cover his tracks."

"Why would Michael want to go back to him?"

"It's all he knows," she'd said. Her wire-rimmed glasses were propped on her thumb and forefinger as she rubbed the inside corners of her eyes. "In a way, it's home, what's familiar. And I'm sure the father knew how to manipulate the boy's feelings. A small kindness here and there, it does wonders. Almost any little thing will make a child feel loved. Particularly if it's relief from abuse."

"The Stockholm syndrome." This was what Dr. Allison had said, too.

"Oh very much that, I suspect," Sister Kathrin said, re-adjusting her glasses to the bridge of her nose. "I'll tell you what else. And this is another one of my guesses. Don't think the boy is going to help you. These sort of children can be fiercely protective of the very people who hurt them —who hold them captive. I've seen this type of behavior many times. Or enough times to know it's true."

"LIFETIME ACHIEVEMENT AWARD my ass." Mother is trying on her fourth Little Black Dress. This one comes three or so inches above the knee. The woman still has very shapely legs but her skin is pale and there are clusters of dark blue veins on her thighs and calves. "It's the kiss of death," Mother says, meaning her award. She has said this before; recently, once or twice a day. "First they give you the award *then* they want to know why you don't spend more time with your family. 'Time is precious,' they tell you. You can't believe the BS. I mean if it's so precious, why don't they spend more time with *their* damn family?"

The rain hasn't quit; it's been raining all day, that soft pat-pat on the window glass. I'm still sitting on the edge of Mother's bed but now I'm staring at the window and the darkness and the tiny wash of lights. It's very difficult to look at Mother in that skimpy dress without feeling embarrassed. She is getting the Old Person Award – her words, not mine – and she's trying to dress like she doesn't deserve it.

"I'm going to bed," I say.

"Do you like the outfit, or what?"

"...very nice."

"So just 'very nice.' That's it?"

"Good night, Mother."

I walk from the bedroom and down the hall. I can only take so much of Mother and her battles. I mean excuse me but I have battles of my own. Right now I'm thinking about Michael and Carlos, Jr. And as I walk the hallway – a passage of shadow and dull yellow light – I make a pledge to myself. I will never be like my father. I will never give up, and I will never turn away from my child or children who need me.

...I promise ... I promise.

I'm thinking about Michael, too. We have so many things in common, Michael and I. Other people have told us who we were and what we had done. We were very young and at the mercy of storytellers, and we believed it all.

@wren&me1 When we 1ˢᵗ met, Wren was a child like me. But she was not like me. When we 1ˢᵗ met, I was afraid and had no place to hide.

FIFTEEN

ON SATURDAY NIGHT my mother calls me from the broadcaster's dinner at the Crowne Plaza Hotel – her Lifetime Achievement Award dinner – and tells me she can't find Carlos, Jr. *Cannot find him.* She says it the way you'd say, "I can't find my necklace. You know, the pearls? Have you seen that, Rhea?" *Cannot find him.* Very calm, very matter-of-fact. Nothing ruffles Dr. Betty. My son had agreed to be his grandmother's dinner date. I'd mixed feelings about this from the start. But he liked the idea of being in a room with a lot of radio people. My poor little boy. Where was my mind? Why do I continue to trust this woman?

"But don't you worry, Rhea. I'm sure he's around the hotel somewhere. You know boys. They're always doing the unexpected."

"How about sounding a little more upset." I couldn't believe the attitude.

"I've looked in the bathrooms, in the kitchen."

I heard no emotion, no nothing. Why not some sobbing, a few unintelligible words? I want her seated at a bar on one a lovely wood stools, her mascara trailing darkly from eye to chin, an elbow resting on a white marble table top.

"I told hotel security," she says.

"...oh Mother." My eyes got hot with tears.

WHEN I FIRST saw Wren, I was four or maybe five

– a year either way – and very alone and very frightened. A little girl in the bedroom with the sheet pulled to her chin, that had been Yours Truly. I haven't forgotten that fear. It's how I was trembling earlier in the evening when Mother told me about Carlos, Jr. I trembled as though I was chilled down to the bone and nothing could thaw me. He has such an open heart, my sweet boy. Like most kids, he wears his feelings out there for everyone to see. Not that he's a pushover, I don't think that. Look I'm the mother, okay? What do you expect me to say? He's a terrific child. And I'm very scared. I couldn't live with myself if something happened to him.

I don't know whether I'd had a bad dream that night – the night Wren came into my life – or whether the world merely felt too gloomy and empty. But that night Wren had walked from the black far corner of the room and stood by the mahogany chiffonier in front of my bed. She wasn't the Wren we know today, nothing like the hero of my graphic novels, no leather jacket and skinny jeans, no piercings and dark eyeliner. But she did have that F-You attitude, that Ok-Bring-It-On-Bitch thing, an arrogance that found the world naive and amusing and too hypocritical for words. Yes on that long ago night, Wren was not so much a person as a doll. She'd reminded me of a floppy clown with her white cloth stitched face and button eyes, her lips too big and too red.

"Hello, lovey," she said. Very English, right from the start.

I lifted the bed sheet above my nose and even with the bottom edges of my eyes.

I wanted to call out for my mother but I was afraid the doll would hurt me. You can be the friendliest talking rag doll in the world but you'll still freak kids out. Oh. And I heard something on the record player coming from the living room. Music. My mother used to listen to music in the evenings. "That's my favorite time of the day," she would tell me. And on that night – for the first time, I think – the music I'd heard was from my quartet, the strings, the clarinet, the piano, and they were playing Cole Porter's "Anything Goes."

"...how's the girl," Wren had said.

"Dolls don't talk."

"I'm no doll."

MY CELL WAS pressed between my ear and hunched shoulder – Mother and I talking about Carlos, Jr. – and I had begun walking toward my son's bedroom. To see what, I don't know. An empty bed. A day or two of dirty clothes on the floor, I don't know. Maybe I wanted to see if Michael was gone, too.

"He's very inquisitive," I tell my mother. "He likes going off on his own. Once when he was a little boy he left the apartment without telling me. And I mean I looked everywhere. Eventually I found him two blocks away. He'd taken five dollars from my purse and he was buying a hot dog from a street vendor. Just don't panic. I'm sure he's around somewhere." I wasn't sure at all, actually.

"I'm not panicking. Maybe a little."

"Me, too." I felt the heat of my tears against my cheek.

Michael is laying on the tan inflatable mattress next to my son's empty bed. *Oh Michael, are you going to let your uncle hurt my boy? He's your friend now. What sort of friend are you going to be? And he's not smart like you. He doesn't know what it means to suffer, not the way you've suffered. Would you really wish that on someone else, on a friend?*

Moonlight is coming through the window and across the wood floor, a clear split of shadow and silver.

Michael has on white jockeys and a sleeveless summer undershirt. His arms and legs are thick, hairless. This marks the second or third time I've seen him in the dark without bandages. Moonlight covers the left half of his body and the skin is silver from the light but I can also see a grayish tint. Thin old scars and some newer ones pattern his bicep and forearm. What continues to astonish me most is that part of him in the shadow. Had it not been for the jockeys and the sleeveless undershirt the boy would have been invisible – or at least that shadowed side of him. I can make out a very slight outline along the shoulder near his undershirt but certainly not much more than that.

"Rhea? Rhea, dear?" Dr. Betty hadn't left the phone.

"Did you call the police?"

"The hotel people are still looking."

"*Moth*er. Fuck the hotel people."

"I'VE NEVER BEEN afraid of the dark." Wren had told me this the first night we'd talked, so many years ago now. Mother had called her my invisible friend. "Only special children have invisible friends," Mother said. That's when Wren had her clown look, her cloth stitched face with the lips that were too big and too red. I suppose it was how a child might imagine her.

"Nothing scares me," Wren would say, hands on her hips. She liked to strut and brag. "The Worry Creepers don't mess with my dreams, I can tell you."

"Don't talk about them."

"But you know who they are, don't you, lovey?"

"No. I don't know any Worry Creepers."

"Well, well. Somebody's lying."

Another present from Mother. She loved telling me about the Worry Creepers. *Sleep tight*, she'd say after tucking me in and kissing my forehead. *Don't let the*

Worry Creepers get you. The Worry Creepers were part of our goodnight ritual. An advanced version of Don't Let the Bedbugs Bite. All my childhood nights ended the same way. Each night began with a bedtime story that was usually an adventure Daddy had related in a recent letter, or that's what Mother wanted me to think. This would be followed by a talk about Daddy and where he was and what he was doing and how he missed his Betty and his Little Rhea and what we would all do once he came home and we could be a family again. And didn't I know how much Daddy loved and adored me?

"HOW OLD IS the child?" the detective wants to know.

"Twelve."

"Okay let me first tell you this, for children under eighteen, there's no twenty-four hour waiting period. The first forty-eight hours are always most important. What's the name?"

"Carlos," I say. "Carlos Neto Flores, Jr."

"And I'm talking to who?"

"I'm the mother. Rhea Waye."

"All right, Ms. Waye, my name is Detective Georgia Halliday. Do you have a pencil and paper?"

"...yes. Wait, wait ... okay."

"I'm required to tell you my badge number, also my telephone, fax, and report numbers. I'll be doing the initial investigation as well as the follow up. So I'm your contact person. Is this clear?"

"...yes."

I called the police after I hung up on Mother who'd been talking about the value of good hotel security. And I did hang up *on* her. There's definitely something wrong with the woman. I'd been laying on Carlos, Jr.'s empty bed, the moonlight dividing the shadows – cell phone pressed to my ear – and I was now writing down the officer's information with a ballpoint pen on a small yellow pad.

"I'm going to need you to help me," Detective Halliday says. "That's the way it works. We're going to help each other." She's all business but there is a soft edge to her voice. It's as if she's done this many times but still knows and cares why she does it. "Are you there?"

"I'm here, yes."

"Okay. I'll need a picture of Carlos, you can fax or email it to me. I want you to include his height, his weight, any identifying features like glasses, birth marks, braces, piercings, that sort of thing. You should include a description of the clothes he was last wearing."

"...clothes. Okay."

"Let me say something else." Officer Halliday then takes an audible breath and seems to shift her tone to something more personal. "I know you love your boy or you wouldn't be on the phone with me. I know you're overwhelmed. But here is the good news. Most kids are found within twenty-four hours. Either we find them or they just wander on home. I want you to keep that in mind, all right?"

"Yes, ma'am."

"You have friends?"

"I have a mother."

"How is she when it comes to support?"

"It depends on the day."

Already I imagine telling the detective about how Carlos, Jr. helps his mother, how he does that every day. *Please take us seriously, okay, I have a good kid.* That's what I want to say. I want Detective Georgia Halliday to feel what I feel, I want *her* support, her kind words. I want her to know that when I'm feeling down my son entertains me with card tricks or makes microwave popcorn and finds a movie I would like on the TV.

"You need to be part of this, Ms. Waye. Talk to your son's friends, the neighbors, relatives. Okay? Contact anyone who you'd think would've seen him."

I was listening to Georgia Halliday and watching Michael as he slept sprawled across the inflatable mattress near my son's bed.

"We've just moved here," I say. "My son doesn't have friends."

"Classmates, perhaps?"

"Not 'til September. And that can't come soon enough, believe me." I sat upright on the bed, the yellow pad balanced on my knees. "Carlos, Jr. is such a people person. I can be alone and that's fine but not him."

"What about the father?"

"We're separated."

"Check all your calls, Ms. Waye. Fathers love their children, too. I'm not saying Mr. Waye – sorry. Flores. Mr. Flores – stole your child. That's not what I'm saying. But it's been know to happen."

"He's in Chicago."

"Doesn't matter, believe me."

"I don't know. I mean it's Chicago."

"Then check your long distance calls," Officer Halliday says. "And something else. Don't touch anything in your child's room. Just shut the door, okay? We may need to see what's there. Letters, a diary, anything that would give us a sense of what the child was thinking at the time. It's never a good idea to contaminate an area."

Great. Already I'm not helping the situation. I'm about to confess my location and how I have messed with the evidence or clues or whatever you'd call it but

155

Georgia Halliday is obviously going down a list she's said many times before and has gone on to other things.

"Have you checked hospitals? Shelters?"

"...no, not yet. But I will, of course. Whatever I have to do."

"We have to cover all our bases," she says. "And leave flyers with your contact information. You know, in malls, your neighborhood and so on."

I don't think any of this will help my son and the sheer amount of tasks I will have to do has already begun to overwhelm me. I'm sure Detective Halliday is a very thorough person and good at her job – I have no complaints there – but I've never been more frightened. Well that's not completely true. If I think about it, I should've said almost never.

WREN HAD SCARED me bad on that first night, our first meeting. We were still in my bedroom and she was standing in front of the bed beside the chiffonier. Her hands rest on her hips and she walked back and forth with a swagger. Music came from the record player in the living room but it sounded very far away. It was the quartet that played the Cole Porter songs, especially "Anything Goes." That was Mothers favorite. I remember Wren's skinny white cloth legs and her starched blue and yellow pinafore.

"I bet you know the Worry Creepers," she had said, an accusing tone, her head tilted slightly. Her black button eyes and painted on mouth had no expression. "Why pretend you don't? Are you a girl who lies?"

"I'm a very *good* girl."

"The Worry Creepers hide in your closet and under your bed," Wren had said. "They whisper to you at night. And you know that."

"Mama says the Worry Creepers aren't real."

"We know better."

"They don't scare you?"

"Nothing scares me. Want to know why?"

I remembering thinking, *I'm not going to ask why. No, no. Do not ask her anything.* I tried to stay quiet. If I'd been a magician like Grandpa Lester, I would have wished myself away.

Wren looked at me with her empty doll eyes. Her face had started to change, I watched it in the moonlight, the white cloth and the stitching altering itself, reshaping itself. She was becoming a girl like me – that had been my thought – but it was nothing like me. Her skin seemed so glassy. There were also other changes. Her black button eyes had melted into dark holes like the slits in a piggy bank. And the painted-on red mouth became a fleshy smile. Her face kept growing, too. God I remember that like it just happened, all I could see was her face and the moonlight. And when she opened her mouth, her teeth were very white and small and pointed. Then Wren had answered her own Want-to-Know-Why question. She'd said, "Because I scare them before they scare me."

I'M LYING TO Detective Halliday and I know it – maybe not directly, but lying nonetheless. I lie to her by what I don't say, what I leave out. I'm constantly editing my thoughts *No need to say this or that,* I think. Or I say to myself, *If I tell her such and such, it will only confuse the issue.* I have become a name, rank and serial number type of person. And as the Detective recites the Missing Child's "Dos and Don'ts" list, I start to fantasize a more honest conversation.

"The man's name is Edward," I'd say, the beginning of my pretend discussion with Georgia Halliday. I would tell her how I believe Edward took my son. Not every detail, mind you, but enough to point a finger. Then I'd say, "I don't know his exact address but I can show you where he lives. It's in the Nicetown-Tioga area. Not the most attractive spot in the world, I realize."

"...Nicetown-Tioga." I imagine Georgia muttering the name. Like she's writing it down. I pictured her taking notes à la Dr. Allison but for very different reasons. These notes will be used for future interrogations. "Do you have a last name for Edward? How do you know him?"

"...what?"

"How do you know him?"

"What does that have to do with anything?" Even in an imagined conversation I get defensive. I'm intimidated easily. But in my fantasy I tell the truth. I tell her, "I thought Edward was my father – it's crazy, I know – but I don't think that anymore. It was a whatever, a brief misunderstanding."

"I'll need some clarification," Detective Halliday says. I hear a change in her voice, an Is This Woman Sane type of change. "How does a person mistake a stranger for a father? How does that happen again?"

"I get your confusion, Detective. I understand completely." I wanted to picture myself laughing everything away. But I am too apologetic and too self-conscious and I stumble around in my own embarrassment. I am not a socially smooth person; I have too many bumps and angles. I don't do glib. Or I don't do it well. Then I'd say, "That's a very good point, Detective. I recognize that mistaking a stranger for a father isn't a usual dilemma. I know what you're saying – implying, I mean."

"Okay. Then enlighten me."

Georgia Halliday's talk has become quiet, soft. It is the sort of voice you use with an emotionally delicate individual. It's how nurses talk to mental patients. *Here come your pilly-pills. Open wide. Wider. WIDER. That's it! Here comes the airplane into the hanger.* Just, you know, kill me.

"Oh listen absolutely," I would say. "You're a professional. You're a busy person. We're both busy people, I get it."

"Uh-huh. Take you're time."

"I believe he's torturing his dead brother's child."

"...pardon?"

"Edward. I also believe the father did it, too."

"...torturing the child."

"That's correct," I'd say.

"And you have proof?" I had pictured Detective Halliday going from polite and supportive to polite and skeptical. "That's a must in these situations, proof's a must. We can't just run on guesses and good will. No doubt you understand that. If you're telling me that Edward What's-His-Name is torturing a child – torturing his nephew – then I'm going to need a shit load of proof. And you have that, I'm presuming? I'm assuming you have everything but eight by ten glossies. What say you, Ms. Waye? Am I right here? Do you have a shit load of evidence for me?"

"No. No, not at the moment. But both of them – the brothers – tortured this boy.

Others also think this is true – one other, but a very reliable person. A nun. A very nice and reliable nun. And Edward's still doing it, I'm almost positive. I think it was a family thing. People tell me it's often a family thing."

"...but you have no proof."

"Not currently, no."

See this is what I mean, precisely: I don't do well with either my fantasies or my real life. Now I'm truly embarrassed. It doesn't matter that I'm making this talk up. I still can't bring myself to tell Detective Halliday how I kidnapped the nephew to protect him. I know I discussed it with Sister Kathrin and I know we now have social services involved, I know all of it. But I cannot shake feeling that I am a criminal, a kidnapper. And I'd have tell the detective that – I'd have to give the details – because me rescuing Michael from what was so obviously a hideous situation is why Edward stole my son.

As I'm imaging this conversation with Detective Halliday, I start to hear her, the *actual* woman. Apparently my silence has been noticed.

"...hello? Hello?" she's saying. "Ms. Waye? Are you there? Did I loose you?"

@wren&me1 Guns, Wren says. Don't u love guns? Guns get u what u want. Dr. Allison says, Wren only knows what u tell her to know.

SIXTEEN

ABOUT AN HOUR and a half ago I called Mother again.

"Where are we with this," I said.

"Where are we with what?"

"My *son*. You're *grand*son."

"You don't have to shout."

It was 12:36 in the morning and she hadn't left her Lifetime Achievement Award dinner at the Crowne Plaza. At that time I'd been in her bedroom looking for her pistol. I held my cell with one hand and weeded through the things in her pine bleached bureau. I remembered Carlos, Jr. telling me about a pistol – I'm sure he told me – but I can't remember where it was supposed to be and I didn't want to ask my mother and have a situation.

"Security is still looking for him," she said, meaning my son.

"I called the police."

"Don't you think that's premature?"

"It's the first forty-eight hours," I'd said. Mother stayed quiet. I'm sure she didn't get what I was talking about and I tried to clarify the situation. "There's less chance of finding him after forty-eight hours. Chances diminish, statistically. That's what the officer told me."

"Listen I'm just as upset as you are, dear." Mother's words were slurred but ever so slightly. I suspected a Chablis or two. "Everybody's looking, you know. It's a very big hotel."

"Where do you keep the pistol?"

"What pistol?"

"Don't do that, okay? Just tell me."

See. Try to get an answer.

"I want you to calm down," Mother said. She whispered this into the phone as if passer-byes at the Crowne Plaza were looking at her and arching their eyebrows.

"I need to go get my son."

"Take a deep breath, dear."

MICHAEL WALKS INTO my mother's bedroom, eyes squinting at the overhead brightness. As he leaves the shadowy hallway and goes into the lighted room the color of his skin alters from dark to pale gray. He has on jockeys and a sleeveless t-shirt and there are many scars on his arms and his legs, particularly the arms, and the newer ones look shiny where I'd rubbed the ointment.

I'm still looking for the damn pistol.

"I woke you, didn't I?"

"...it's okay."

Most of Mother's things from the bureau are now on the teal carpeted floor, bras, panties, sweaters, silky little tops. Her closet has been cleaned out, too. Shoes and shoe boxes are pretty much everywhere. Mother's clothes are on their hangers and piled atop the bed. I am determined to find this pistol. I know it's here; Carlos, Jr. would have no reason to lie. And I can just picture Mother telling him about it. She tells my son stuff she'd *never* tell me. But so far I have only found items I feel too embarrassed to discuss. I'll mention them in passing, very quickly. A magazine of naked men, for one. A pink vibrator the size of a zucchini, for another. I mean everyone – if they want it – should have some type of sex life. I'm not talking about pet sex or that sort of thing. But this is my mother. My *mother*. What is wrong with her?

"Are you all right?" I say to Michael.

"Where's Carlos?"

"I don't know, sweetie." I give him the best No Worry smile I have. No sense getting the boy upset. "He was at the hotel with his grandma, that broadcaster's dinner. But he's wandered off – which is typical Carlos, believe me. He's got antsy pants bad. I'm sure things are fine."

"You think it's my uncle." He says this in a small clear voice.

"I think he was very angry, don't you?"

"He didn't want me to go."

"Weren't you being hurt?"

"Uncle Edward's a good person," the boy says. His eyes are still squinted, a hand cupped above his brow to block the light. He steps back into the hallway and shadows.

I think Michael feels more relaxed when there is no light. "Edward took me in when I had nobody. They were going to give me to foster care. He said I could stay as long as I wanted."

"But your uncle *did* hurt you." I wasn't letting him slip by that.

"People have moods."

"YOU'RE WAY TOO upset for firearms," she'd said.

"It's my son, Mother. Carlos – remember him? Your *date*? I mean do you think I just blithely pulled this anger out of my ass?"

"You'd be killing the first person who annoys you." She had her unruffled therapist's voice. God I hate that.

"Thanks for your confidence."

I was on my hands and knees in her bedroom closet

– the cell phone between my shoulder and tilted head – tossing out whatever was there in front of me, shoes, a sewing basket, leather bound photo albums, you name it. Every-so-often I would stop and try to recall what my son had said about the pistol, where he said Mother kept it. But I knew I was thinking about where it might be too much; and when I do that, nothing happens. I have to put my mind on other things, irrelevant things, then it will come to me. Right now, though, it's hard to gather my thoughts.

"I don't want you harming yourself, either," Mother said. And I don't know why but I believe her. Actually I *do* know why. The woman is bothered by my past behavior.

"You don't trust me," I said.

I was peering into the black corners of the closet. I need an f-ing flashlight, okay? I never have the right tools. You know how some people always have the right tools for the right job? Oh let me fix this squeak in this door. Let me repair the garbage disposal. Or build a bird house. What*ever*. Well I don't have a tool to my name. This is a big part of my problem: I am a person alienated from the things I need to fix other things.

I should talk to Dr. Allison about that.

"Have you given me reason to trust you?" Mother says.

"Pardon? Do I have to?"

"It wouldn't hurt."

I'm waiting for her rant on how I took a kitchen knife to the sofa. This was where our conversations about trust usually end up – me, a knife and living room furniture.

"Give these people a chance," Mother said, meaning the hotel security. "You've been here in the Crowne Plaza, it's enormous. You don't think these people know their business, these security people?

Believe me, they know."

"It's my child, Mother. I can't just sit by."

"I'm not a fool, I understand that," she'd said. Those glasses of Chablis had made her more talkative than I'm used to. "You want to believe that I don't love your Carlos. You've got no idea about a grandmother and her grandson. You know nothing about that sort of love. I see you in his face, Rhea. He has your eyes, your mouth. I remember you when I see him, when you were my girl. That what grandparents see. They see their own in the eyes of their children's children. That's something you don't know. You're too young to know that. You are too young to know how much more there is to this life."

"I'm hanging up now."

"Yes you do that. That's so you."

"Good-bye, Mother."

"You don't know how to think."

"...excuse me?"

"Or you don't want to." Her words had come out scrunched. *Youdunwannathink*. This was followed by a metallic click and a very audible exhale.

"Are you smoking?"

"Shoot first, think later – you and the Lone Ranger, my Rhea and the Mask Man. You have a coward's rage. 'I don't know what to do but get angry,' that's what you say. It's a dangerous way to go through life, dear."

"I thought you quit smoking."

"You keep underestimating me."

I LIKE THE moonlight in Carlos, Jr.'s room. It's shimmering silver and crosses the wood floor and Michael's inflatable mattress; crosses my son's empty bed, too. Michael is on the mattress, hands behind his head, looking beyond the partially open window at the moon.

"You're awake," I say. It hasn't been the best of nights for him, either.

"You're going to my house." It's a statement.

"I'm thinking about it."

The boy's left shoulder and the foot and calf of his left leg are in the moonlight, the skin luminous gray. The rest of him lays in the darkness and very close to invisible.

I imagine he'd have no problem hiding himself. Had it not been for the dog collar and chain, a basement would've been the perfect place for disappearing. I'm sure the father and the uncle never unleashed him. Without it, I can see these two brothers wooing and threatening the boy for hours. *Show yourself, sonny! We know you're here, don't think we don't!* Michael owes a lot to his aunt's faulty genetics. We never know what will be a blessing, do we? She'd given him an odd sort of salvation, or the possibility of it.

"You've been nice to me," Michael says. "You and Carlos. Carlos says I'm the invisible boy. He thinks I'm like Wren, that I'm a super hero. It's embarrassing but I like it, too. Carlos says he wants me to teach him how to be invisible."

"That's sounds like him." I suddenly feel very sad when I say that and I want to go off some place and melt into tears. It's as if I am talking about the memories of my son, as if he were a dead person.

"Uncle Edward wouldn't hurt your son," Michael says. "I don't know if Carlos is there but if he is, Uncle Edward will just keep him until he gets me back."

"He hurt you all the time."

"That was my fault. I kept doing stuff that upset him."

I picture Dr. Allison wanting to know why I have attached myself to Michael. I hear her saying, "I understand your concern for his suffering. But this is different, isn't it? Something additional, more powerful than the obvious."

I don't know, what do I say to that?

I *feel* the darkness of Michael's basement. I smell the damp air and the hard dirt of the floor. And rotting fruit, I smell that, too – apples, mostly the sweet rotting smell of apples. I know this place more than I have known anything else in my life. There are the scratchy sounds of things alive but unseen. Cobwebs catch his hair, his face. Others walk above him and talk and clear their throats and lives their lives but it is all so far away, all so irrelevant to him. Michael has lived in that, year after year. His father's basement, his uncle Edward's basement: this is what he knows, Sister Kathrin is right. He's a very lonely boy. Maybe that's it, I can feel his emptiness. That darkness, that emptiness, I feel it and smell it and know it too well.

"TELL ME WHERE," I say. I've called Mother back one final time. Hotel security has yet to find Carlos, Jr. and I am totally frustrated. "I need that pistol. You don't want your daughter going into a situation unprotected."

"I don't want you in a situation, period."

"It's my son, Mother."

"Listen I love that boy, too. You think I don't love my own grandson? But you talked to the police. Now let them do the job."

"This isn't like you have a vote, okay?"

I'm sitting on the edge of her bed and glancing about the room. Bureau drawers are pulled out, the contents of the drawers scattered about the carpeted floor. The same is true of the closet. Underwear, slips, sweaters, shoes, photo albums, the place has that post tornado look.

"...Rhea," Mother sounds worn, tired. "I bought that gun years ago. Fifteen, twenty years. I think I had target practice with it once. I don't know if the damn thing works, okay? Have you ever fired a weapon?"

"My ex taught me."

"What ex? You're not divorced."

"My *estranged* husband, whatever you want to call him." I have no intention of getting intosemantics with a woman who has been going at the Chablis and smoking cigarettes.

"That's certainly closer to the truth."

"He left *me*, Mother. For Ivy Landis."

"...who?"

"Some woman, a realtor."

"Men don't know what they want." Mother is huffing on another cigarette, I can hear her inhaling. Give her wine and her resolve cracks like cheap China. "Believe me, Rhea, I know men. Ask my listeners – Dr. Betty knows – these women rely on me regularly. It's always a contest between the little head and the big head. That's the tragedy of being a man."

"The pistol, please. *Where's* the pistol." At this point it's more a belligerent command than a question.

"All I need is you shooting somebody. Or worse, yourself."

"Forty-eight hours, Mother. Then our chances begin to stink. C'mon."

"...Rhea, please. I don't want to loose you both. I'm not as strong as you think. Or as I think." Her voice has turned thick and there's a quiver to it. "I don't understand. What can you do that the police can't? You know what I mean, these people are trained. It's their job, they do it every day. You draw your books. I do my program. They do crime things. Everybody has their job."

I always want my mother to care about me and I

always think she's too involved with herself to care about anything. Then I hear her voice getting all squishy and halting and I want her to quit that and go back to being the self-centered Dr. Betty I know and resent. I find I don't like all that caring, that mushiness, it creeps me out. I'm far more comfortable being indignant.

"It isn't reliable," she says. The pistol, I mean. It's old like me, that pistol. I don't do maintenance on it, or whatever you're supposed to do. Oil it, I don't *oil* it. Or take it all apart and wipe down each little piece. It's too much like a fetish."

"We can discuss this later."

"I'm just saying. It's not the best."

"Where, tell me *where*."

"...the nightstand." It's a reluctant whisper.

Shit. Of course.

I remember Carlos, Jr. telling me that. The *night*stand. I tear apart an entire room and it's right there in the nightstand. And that's exactly where I'd put it, I'd put it next to me, where I could get my hands on it. Why don't I pay more attention to that child? See this is why Carlos, Jr. got into this crap in the first place. He has a self-absorbed parent who can't put two and two together.

"Is she young?" Mother says.

"...pardon?"

"This Ivy Landis. Is she young?"

"There all young, Mother."

"Boy, that's the truth."

I open the mahogany nightstand drawer and there's the pistol. Carlos, Sr.'s pistol was a Beretta and this one is also a Beretta – I see that three arrow logo on the grip – but it's a smaller pistol, what people call a sub-compact. It fits in the palm of my hand. And

I hate to say it's cute but it is, you know. Very cute

and sleek and I like the way the hard
    rubber grip feels in my hand. I aim it at a shadowed
corner of the bedroom and whisper
    the word, *kapow*. I can't help but laugh. What can
I say, the word amuses me. I love
    that word and I've used it more than once in my
Wren novels.
    Kapow! Kapow!
    "Rhea? Baby? Hello?" Mother's voice is so far
away.
    Kapow!

@*wren&me1* I'm different, Wren says. U r 2 distant. But u r always with me, I tell her. And it's a surprise 2 speak that and 2 think that.

SEVENTEEN

I GOT THE BROAD Street subway at City Hall. It's 2:12 AM and an older guy and I are the only two people in the car. A light in the car is about to go out and it's been snapping and blinking above us. There's an overly sweet disinfectant smell and I feel the train shake as it goes through the darkness. The older guy doesn't look all that well. His khakis are grimy and he has on a worn fatigue jacket, circa Vietnam, '72, '73, somewhere around there. He could be a vet or he could've bought the jacket at a surplus store. Or perhaps he stole it off a poor dead soldier. I don't know what his actual name is but I've decided to call him Stanley. When I was a kid I used to make up names and stories about subway people but I haven't thought much about doing that since I left Philadelphia. That's what this town does. My childhood waits for me here.

Stanley's hair is gray and over his ears and sort of greasy, I think he's very down on his luck. He also has on one of those hunting caps with the ear flaps. So Crazy Vet, that's my fantasy. Maybe a druggie. Switched from heroin to methadone sometime in the eighties or early nineties but he goes back from time to time and reminisces – rub that vein, shoot that shit. He likes drifting off and imagining the jungle. Our Stanley has that Ready to Nod look but he sees me and smiles. His small teeth are dark about the edges. I smile back at him. My right hand is inside the pocket of my black leather jacket, fingers clutching Mother's pistol.

"YOU'RE DRESSED LIKE Wren," Michael said. He seemed genuinely taken back. This was just before I had left the house to get the subway. "You have everything but the little earrings. She really *is* you."

"Oh that's not true."

It is true, of course. More than one reviewer has called Wren my "alter ego." And my answer is usually, "There's nothing 'alter' about it."

"You should go look at yourself," Michael said.

He was sitting on the tan inflatable mattress, legs crossed Indian style. Moonlight showed most of his body. There is a fishy smell from the ointment I'd used on his newer wounds. The skin appeared gray and luminous but swatches of him were lost to the shadows, a knee, a left shoulder.

"You like Wren." I knew he did.

"Yeah. She's not afraid of anything."

"But she's a fiction, you know. Something I made up."

"I still like her," he said, a little embarrassed. "And you and her could be twins, Miss Waye. I mean it as a compliment."

"I know, hon. You need to sleep now."

When I was dressing earlier I hadn't thought much about it. I'd merely grabbed stuff from my closet. But at some point I did look in the mirror – my mother's full length mirror – and I'd thought the same thing Michael had just said. They were unconscious choices, believe me. What I had grabbed were my skinny black jeans, my hightops and a black waist-length jacket. It was only after I was dressed and looked at myself in the mirror did I realize what I'd done. *God, I'm her.* I was stunned, I do admit that, the way Michael had been stunned when he saw me dressed this way. Yet it's like so many other times in my life. Things happened after-the-fact. It can be the sketches I know I've done but don't remember the actual act of doing them. Or a more simple thing like hearing my Dinner Music Quartet playing Cole Porter's "Anything Goes" as I'm drawing Wren and it not occurring to me that Mother played the song on the night Wren first appeared in my bedroom. As I think about it now, why wouldn't a childhood song come back again and again?

THERE ARE FOUR of them – three black guys and a very pale white guy, but I'm thinking one of the black guys is a Puerto Rican or a Dominican – big boys, maybe high school football, though one looks more a basketball type. They get on at the North Philly stop. The polished steel doors make a *woosh!* and the boys don't walk into the car as much as explode into it – loud kids, pushing one another, laughing, their heads covered in hoodies and baseball caps. A red Phillies one; an Orioles, too.

One of the lights in the car is still blinking and making a buzzing noise. The light is very bright and gives the kids a washed out look. Along with that, they have loaded on the Polo cologne – or whatever the brand, something strong – and the cologne mixes with the disinfectant smell of the car.

The taller boy sees Stanley hunched in his plastic seat, his shoulders ear level, not looking at anyone and not wanting to be seen. Stanley's lips are moving, his eyes have no focus and he is in Stanley World. That's what I'm thinking. And I'm thinking he must go to Stanley World whenever he hears things that frighten him.

"Hey, hobo," the tall boy says.

Then the others get in it.

"*Hey* hobo."

"S'up, hobo."

"Ho-*bo*!"

The four boys laugh at each other. They are their own best audience. Big goofy boys doing goofy shit. Everything is very funny to them, that's how they're seeing this. A regular laugh riot. Like nobody has ever thought of harassing a junkie before. Such clever little children. They can smell Stanley's weakness. Finally an adult they can slap around instead of being slapped around. Oh I get it, I just don't like it.

Already I'm not thrilled with them.

"Guy's fuckin' whacked, you know?" the boy in the Orioles cap says. He's the very pale white boy. He has a hint of a mustache that's more visible at the edges of his lip than the middle of it.

"You need to film this shit, LaMar." the tall one says.

"This is YouTube."

"Let me see teeth, hobo. Smile." LaMar is shorter and wider than the others and he's wearing thick black framed glasses.

"Yeah get them green teeth."

LaMar already has his iPhone out, recording Stanley World live. He's got1080p

HD. He's got 8 megapixels and that Edit as You Go stuff – on the fly, on the sly, all the

time. He saying that as he's filming; giving his boys the stats, what the phone's got, what it can do.

"Phone do everything but suck my dick," LaMar says.

"What dick?" Two boys say this simultaneously.

It's Stanley World, a pop away from becoming viral.

"YOU CALLED YOUR uncle?" I'd just finished saying goodnight to Michael when he told me about talking to Edward that afternoon. "On what? You don't have a have a cell."

"I borrowed yours. I wanted you to know."

"Uh-huh. And where exactly was I?"

I couldn't believe it. I'm trying to protect this boy from God knows what sort of abuse and he's talking to the very guy who's been abusing him. You can't make it up. But Sister Kathrin says this is what happens. Dr. Allison has said it, too. The Stockholm Syndrome. All I know about that is Patty Hearst holding up a bank with the SLA in '74, that was supposed to be Stockholm – siding with her captors when daddy only gave six million to buy food for the San Francisco poor. I know I don't listen to people. That's how I am, it's a major fault. Tell me you're an expert and I go deaf. What else would you expect the daughter of Dr. Betty to do? I'm thirty-nine years old and I'm still having authority issues.

"Where was I?" I said again, talking about Michael using my cell.

"I dunno – working, I guess."

"Look at the scars on your arms. The man hurt you."

"But I have bad habits," the boy said. He was standing by the bedroom window.

Moonlight showed the gray skin of his face and arms. "I'm always doing things without consulting him. He *is* my guardian. Uncle Edward's right, I need to put myself in his place, see it from – what-you-call-it – his point of view and all."

I didn't want to get angry but I felt myself wanting to shake him. *Be logical*, I'd thought. *Step back and see what you're doing*. Instead of this being about his uncle as one of the men who abused him, the boy thought of himself as someone who continually frustrated a man who had his best interest at heart. I don't know how to fight that. How do I get Michael to think about his life, how do I help? I have respect for Dr. Allison, I'll tell you that. I know what it's like to work against my own interest and not have a clue. Michael and I are more alike than different. And the doctor's right, this isn't my job. I understand that. But Carlos, Jr. is in trouble and I need to deal with it.

"What time did you call?" I'd said.

"Noon, one. I'm not sure."

"Michael, I'm not angry, okay?"

"You sound angry."

"Maybe angry at myself, maybe that." I'm more frightened than angry but the boy doesn't have to know everything.

STANLEY HAS HIS head down and an open hand is beneath the brim of his cap to block the camera. The florescent tube that was blinking and making noise just burned out. There are shadows in the car now and a dark space along the long strip of overhead lights. But Stanley hasn't noticed any of it.

LaMar is telling him to take his hand away. "Hey you ruinin' my shot, man.

What's wrong wit you? You don't ruin a man's shot." Then to the tall boy, "Hey tell this fool he's ruining my shot."

"C'mon, c'mon," the tall boy says to Stanley. "We're going to make you famous. I know you want to be famous. You be beatin' away the ladies. You like ladies, right? Am I right? Just think about it, man. They be saying, 'Oh, baby, oh baby.' And you be sayin, 'get away from me bitch.' Or like, 'And go get me a beer.' Or whatever you be drinking. Scotch or whatnot."

"Get you're fuckin' hand down, man," LaMar says. He's moving this way and that, trying to shoot around the man's hand. "How I supposed to do my artistic shit if I got to deal wit this, Dwayne?" Dwayne is the tall guy, apparently. Then LaMar says to Stanley, "You think Mona Lisa was hold her fuckin' hand in front of her face? She *never* did that, man. The bitch knew a good thing. Why you think she's smiling like that? Man, you one ungrateful motherfucker."

"Hey calm down, LaMar."

"I'm just saying. Let me do my job."

"Yeah you gonna fall out," the boy with the Orioles cap says. "It's a wonder you standin' anyways. All that fat."

The train swayed back and forth as it turned a corner and continued on through the darkness. Every once in a while a yellow light would go by the window. I've started feeling nauseated. *God don't let me throw up*. It's the motion of the train – maybe the boys, too. My hand hasn't left my jacket pocket. If I'm holding the pistol, I am safe, or that's what I think. The chances that one of the four boys also has a pistol is good and I don't want to turn a subway ride into *Gunfight at the OK Corral*. Believe me, I am not after a fight. I simply want to get Carlos, Jr. and go home. And where are the cops? Usually they patrol the platforms and the trains; they got dogs and everything.

"Somebody hold his hand down," LaMar is saying. "Jason, get your cracker ass over here and hold this bitch."

Jason is one with the Orioles hat and the almost-mustache. "If he don't want it, he don't want it," Jason says. "Fuck him, LaMar. You got to respect the man's wishes and shit."

Now the fourth boys steps in. This boy hasn't done anything until now. He's a watcher. This one is big and muscular and he's wearing a gray hoodie that hides his face. He grabs Stanley by the front of his worn fatigue jacket and lifts him off the red and white plastic seat with one hand. He shakes him until I think Stanley's brains are going to fall out. But instead of brains I see his khaki's go dark and piss making a pool on the floor below him. I smell it, that piss, that fear.

"Let go," I say. I am already up and the pistol is out. I'm holding it with both hands, arms stiff and straight, aiming it at the big boy who is holding Stanley with one hand. "You. *You.* Let go right now. Don't look at me, do it. Do it right *now.*" The boy could break me in two but he carefully lowers Stanley onto his red and white plastic seat. "Very good, very good. Okay, that's good." I am so anxious I can barely hear my own words. "Now all of you get over there by the door. Do it fucking now, do it *now.*" And they do. This is amazing. I keep the pistol aimed at them. I feel and hear the blood pumping in my neck and ears. "Listen to me," I say. "You listening?"

"Yes, Ma'am." Jason and Dwayne say this together. The big boy who had Stanley by the throat nods.

"Okay, good. Excellent." I stay my ground while the pistol moves from one boy to the other. "When that door opens, everybody's gone. I don't care where you go. I don't care what you do. Seriously, I don't give a fuck. But you're not in my life *and* you're not in his life" – I nod to Stanley. "We understand one another?"

"Yes, ma'am," Dwayne and Jason say.

"Good boys."

"HE'S MY FAMILY, you know. It's just him and me." Michael was still talking about his Uncle Edward.

"I'm aware, very much aware." I couldn't remember drawing my own sketches, why should I fault Michael for believing his uncle had the sort of love somebody would want and treasure? It's the boy's safety that concerns me; my son's safety, too. "What did you say to him? Did you talk about Carlos and his grandmother going to the dinner tonight, the broadcaster's dinner? Think, please. Did you mention anything about that?"

"...yes."

"All right, okay. How did you put it." My hands had started to shake and I folded my arms against my chest to hide them.

"I'm sorry."

"What did you say? How did you put it?"

"I said I had a new friend." Michael looked away from me, toward the bedroom window and the clear moonlit night. I could tell he already knew he'd done something wrong. "You know, that Carlos was my knew friend. That I liked having a friend, somebody my age. I never had a friend before, not another kid. Then Uncle Edward wanted to speak to him."

"...to Carlos?"

"You know, to say hello."

Part of me didn't wanted to hear this. It's one thing to imagine a bad situation; it's another to have it confirmed. And the idea of Edward speaking with my son – that he was able to come into my home and do that, even on a cell – left me with an absolute feeling of helplessness and dread.

"What did you tell him?"

"I said, 'Why do you want to talk with Carlos?' I mean I was the one who called him. Why didn't he want to talk to me?" Michael turned from the window. He wasn't crying but his eyes shined as if the tears were not far off. "You'd think he would be glad to hear from me. To know I was all right, that I hadn't been run over by a truck or hurt or whatever. Uncle Edward always says he doesn't have anybody but me, that the two of us are alone in the world. 'We're all we've got,' he says. But most of the time I don't think he's interested. I keep feeling that I'm going to really upset him one day and he's going to tell me to leave his house."

"We can be your friends," I'd said. I was sitting on the edge of Carlos, Jr.'s bed, watching the boy, the way his skin changed to meet the shadows. "Carlos and me, we're not family, I know it's not the same. But having friends, that's important, too. My son's a good boy, Michael. He can be very loyal. Once he likes you, he likes you forever. He's that's sort of kid, my Carlos."

"He calls me the invisible boy."

"It's a compliment."

"Uh-huh I know." Michael sat down on the inflatable mattress – moonlight surrounding him – elbows resting on crossed legs. "He thinks I'm a super hero. Like Wren."

"Wren *isn't* a super hero."

I had said that too defensively. I think of super heroes as being less than human, a child's invention, a fiction to sooth isolation and fear. Or perhaps they are more than human. They have capes and bright costumes. They are pure justice, pure goodness. Or they are troubled and dark souls but rise above their petty demons. To me, Wren is none of that. She's a person, I see her as a wise sister, a confidante, an instructor, someone to rely on and also someone who isn't frightened to do what should be done.

"But you know she'd fight for you," the boy said. "Isn't that a super hero, the person you want on your side?"

I answered him right away. "What about you, Michael? Tell me what I want to hear. Are you on our side?"

@wren&me1 There comes a time when the end begins. U can't escape it. Conclusions will always be drawn. And Wren didn't say that. I did.

EIGHTEEN

I LEFT THE subway at the Eire station and I'm now making my way down West Hunting Park. The digital time on my cell reads 2:17AM and the night is clear and starry and cool. I am paranoid about those four boys I forced off the subway and I look around to see if they're following me but I'm alone. Nicetown used to be a dangerous place but not so much, anymore. Still. Wise people don't waltz around here at two in the morning.

"Aren't we the brave girl, lovey." Already, she's amused.

"Do I have a choice?"

"So a mother armed and dangerous?"

"...exactly."

I've been carrying on this conversation with Wren to keep myself company – it's what I did as a little girl; Wren's reason to be, so-to-speak – though the conversation is my own back and forth thoughts and not an actual talk. I should also say I'm sure I get too animated once in awhile and probably mumble something out loud. I just hope to God I don't have that crazy person look. I don't want anyone thinking, *isn't that bizarre girl talking to herself?* It's how I get through a stressful situation, I will talk about the problem with Wren. That's the way it's always been, Wren and Yours Truly. She is my pooka and no different than Elwood P. Dowd's Harvey, that six foot one and one half inch rabbit who only Mr. Dowd could see. Dr. Allison says many boys and girls have invisible friends, especially creative types.

"We go back a long time," Wren whispers. "You used to say, 'I don't know what I'd do without you, Wren.' Then you'd say, 'Please don't ever leave. Promise. Promise me and hope to die.' Remember that, lovey? We're the best of friends."

"I was four, maybe five."

Where does a life go? I think.

THIS NEIGHBORHOOD IS very old. I look at the houses and the streets and the stores and I feel the scruffiness of everything. It's happened slowly – particularly for the residents, I'm sure – but there's no doubt about it. Here row houses go on endlessly, one after the other – the weathered brown brick, the chipped and peeled neglect of white trim and gray porches. Each tiny front lawn has a wilted-looking tree and a single boxwood. The boxwood are either severely clipped and shaped into domes and squares or they are overgrown and ragged.

"Why am I so worried?" Wren wants to know. My internal conversation with her hasn't ended, the back and forth of my thoughts. "This must be how you feel," she says. "I don't remember ever being this way – all distraught and beside myself, it's not what I do. Never, never. You're the one who isn't sure of things. Why else would I be here? That's how it is with us, isn't it? I calm you, I give you comfort and instruction. You're not sure and I am always sure."

"...but not tonight?" I know something is wrong, too.

"What is it I'm feeling?"

It's very bizarre to hear her so lost. Disturbing, if you must know. But Wren is right, she helps me; I don't help her. What would be the point in that? I was the troubled and frightened little girl and I had called on her, invented her the way children do. *Come help me. Come keep me company, keep me safe.* And while Mother sipped on a glass of Chablis and played her records in the living room – Cole Porter and our Dinner Music Quartet – I'd invited Wren into my bedroom.

"Can you guess the song?" I say. But I say it in a thought, not out loud. "It was 'Anything Goes,' remember?"

"Our song," she says. And I imagine her smiling.

EDWARD'S FRONT DOOR isn't locked. It's open slightly, an inch or so. I'm standing on the gray wood porch and the wood is split and peeling in spots. Edward isn't taking care of the place, that I can see. The front siding should be replaced, too. I don't know if I noticed this the first time I was here. Or maybe I did but now the place has a more worn look, an eerier feel to it.

"...why the open door?" I can barely make out my own words.

The answer is immediate "You know why." It's Wren; her voice a thought that slips about me. "Who taught him to fight? Our boy, our Carlos? Who taught him about the world and what to do?"

I remembered the sketches of Wren and my son running the rooftops. One sketch had Carlos leaping from the roof and falling into Wren's open arms.

"You taught him," I say.

"Think again."

I don't know what to say to that. There were other sketches. One had Wren and Carlos, Jr. squatting at the edge of a roof at night, Wren tapping a knife at the concrete ledge between her feet. Those large dark birds that watched my father in the desert were also perched on the roof, their scarlet faces and skinny necks, their golden eyes. Below Wren and my son there was the man with the cane. He walked near the shadows of the buildings, his cane bumping out a rhythm against the sidewalk.

"You taught him how to hunt," I say.

"I taught him nothing. That was you, Rhea. You didn't run the roofs but you kept him strong. You understand the job mothers have to do."

I'm about to protest but stop.

Yes I *know* that's true. Of course it's true. I understand what is real and what fantasies I decide to entertain. Dr. Allison likes to tell me how I give every feeling that makes me uncomfortable to Wren, particularly the aggressive ones, the angry ones. Let Wren deal with, that's been my motto for years. And knowing all the while that it's pretend. It's what I did as a child. *You say that, Wren. And I'll say this. I'll be the good girl and you say the naughty things.* Yet here I am tonight with a gun in my pocket and looking for my kid.

THE SKY IS still dark and clear, the night air cool, even a bit chilled. Both hands are in the pockets of my leather jacket. The fingers of my right hand rests on the handle and barrel of Mother's pistol. There's a strong electrical smell coming from the house. I don't know what, exactly – burnt wiring.

"...hello? Anybody?"

Silence.

I open the door and step inside but I refuse to close the door behind me. I like it open; I like knowing I can turn and run without anything between me and the street. The living room is filled with shadow but florescent lights flicker and hum in the kitchen. My stomach goes tight, a knot the size of a baby fist. The TV screen is fractured into a perfectly centered cobweb.

Next to the TV, the glass in the gun case is busted up, too. But the shotgun inside the gun case remains untouched, thank God.

The living room looks as if cattle had stampeded through it. Both mahogany end tables are overturned and the lamps that were on the tables are shattered. Edward's big recliner is on its back, stubby legs pointing at the TV. Magazines and newspapers that were stacked in two neat piles by the recliner have been scattered about the floor. The small dining room isn't much different. Two high back caned chairs are knocked over and lay on their sides near a table. Along with that, a framed oil painting is on the floor, it's glass cracked. There's a square space where the picture had been, a shade lighter than the wall's beige painted surface.

"Carlos is putting up a fight," Wren tells me.

Imagination and anxiety are in overdrive. I feel my legs dissolving and I lean the flat of my hand against the dining room wall for balance. I think I see Wren in a dark far corner – she's always in one dark corner or another – but I know it's me wishing she was an actual person I could count on, an extra gunslinger.

"Maybe Carlos *is* at the hotel," I say.

"You know that's not true."

"BUT I HELPED you, didn't I?" Wren doesn't sound like herself, I can't stop thinking that. Her confidence is falling apart and I'm not used to hearing the anxiety. I suppose I should say I've never pretended she needed any reassurance until now – that would be more accurate. And this isn't a good time for me to make her all squishy and sensitive. Then Wren says, "I showed you how not to be afraid, how to do things. I've been quite helpful, lovey. You have to admit it."

I'm in the kitchen and I've opened the door to the

basement. I look down at the shadowed steps. The steps disappear into blackness and I can't see much of anything. A tiny window down there does bring a bit of moonlight but the glass is dirty and the light is too dull to see anything. I remember an overhead light bulb being in the basement. It switches on by pulling a thin cord attached to the bulb's receptacle. That means I have to go down these wood steps in the dark – and believe me, it's *major* darkness – and pull a stupid cord. You would think Edward would have better electrical solutions.

"We were both so young," Wren is saying. She's trudging down memory lane. It's strictly thoughts and not words but I must be keeping her chatty to stop obsessing too much about what I have to do and what might happen if I don't do it. I've no desire to dwell on some man hurting my Carlos. "You couldn't have managed without me," Wren says, very British, very crisp. "I was the strong one, lovey. You know that. I was the one who never let you down. Isn't that so? Let me hear you say it."

"Stop being so anxious," I whisper.

"I don't get anxious."

"Of course you do. Everybody does."

"Let me hear you say it." She won't give up. I believe I feel her breath close to my ear but I know that's impossible. "...go on. Say it."

"You never let me down."

It's a fall from Grace, isn't it? To hear her this way. Wren has always been my protector, my instructor, my confidant. Recently, I've been saying that to myself over and over. Protector. Instructor. Confidant. It's what I'd wanted her to be; it's what she gave me. Or I gave myself, I don't know. It was certainly real at the time. And I liked that reality, it helped me get along, it helped me get to sleep. Dr. Allison says Wren was the father I never had.

"But she's a girl," I told Allison.

"It's the attitude, not the sex."

Mother was depressed for many years, I realize that. After reading my father's letter, I wonder if she did not blame me for their break up. If the shoe had been on the other foot, if my mother and I could have changed places, maybe I would've blamed her. *Thanks to you, your father left.* Oh I know me and I am sure I'd have blamed her. It's too easy to go there. And I'm sure she did it with me.

What I remember were the shadows in my bedroom. And shadows are shadows, no different that the ones at the end of these stairs; the shadows in the basement with the light bulb you have to switch on by pulling a cord. Five or ten minutes after my mother kissed me goodnight, the record player would start. The music seemed distant to me but it came from the living room and was closer than I allowed myself to think. The Dinner

Music Quartet played Cole Porter night after night. "Anything Goes," that was her song, or *their* song. I believe things got very bad for Mother – I was a little girl but little girls know these things – and I was afraid I'd lose her, too. Funny how this works, not ha-ha funny but serious funny. The night I first thought about losing Mother was also the night Wren strutted into my bedroom with her cloth face and her stitched on smile. She was no more than a girl-doll then. I'd thought Wren and I could keep Mother from wandering into the desert to find my father. Wren and I could stop her from becoming another meal for the birds with scarlet faces and white beaks and wide black wings.

WHERE ARE YOU, Carlos? Right now I'm feeling frantic; if my son isn't in this house, I can't imagine where he'd be. *I know you're here. What has he done*

with you? You tried to get away, I know you did. That's what I saw upstairs, isn't it? Did you get him angry?

I had switched on the light blub a minute or two ago and the bulb is still swinging above me, a slow drift of light and shadow as it steadies itself. The gray dirt floor is a bit uneven and the basement smells of earth and piss. Nobody's here. *Nobody.* And I'm not sure what I'm supposed to do now, where I'm supposed to go. *Jesus, Carlos, where are you?* There is a metal army cot in the corner of the room. The olive green blanket folded about the mattress in neat hospital corners. Next to the foot of the bed are two wooden bins. Coal fills one of the bins; potatoes and onions are in the other. What I don't see is a chair and leather collar, not on the bed, not anywhere. Sister Kathrin is right. Social services had gone into this place and they didn't find a collar and chain, either. I swear I remember those horrible things on the cot.

"May be you imagined it," Wren says.

"I know what I saw."

"You can be wrong, you're not perfect." My thoughts have been nothing but this dialog between Wren and I since I stepped off the subway. "That's your trouble lately," she's saying. "You've become very stubborn, lovey. Quite impossible, really."

"Well feel free to leave."

"...what did you say?"

What am I doing?

I said those words before I could stop them. And it doesn't matter that I said the comment to myself. Whether my words are spoken to others or to me, once these words enter the firmament they stay there until the end of the universe, the end of time. They're *I Love Lucy* reruns in space, but not as funny, not as endearing. Lucy, Ricky, Fred and Ethel float in the darkness forever. One day an alien race light years from us will come upon the words *Honey I'm home* and great alien minds will apply for grants to ponder the meaning. Myths wait to be fashioned; religions wait to be formed. And these great alien minds will believe the secret of life has been given to them by advanced beings from space.

Honey, I'm home.

What does this mean? If only the mystery could be unravel.

I don't underestimate what I say to myself – not anymore, I don't. My scoldings, my throwaways. These thoughts are camouflaged but occasionally insightful, a rabbit pulled from a hat I'd no idea I owned. *Ah-ha! Oh-oh!* I think. There is no pretending I didn't say it; no taking it back, either. There's no delete button. *Oh excuse me, did I say that? What I meant was* – un-huh, sorry. I don't get to do that. That's the price people pay for being an adult. These talks between Wren and I are truly between me and me. And I've known that long before my sessions with Dr. Allison. Wait. Another symptom of adulthood is to give credit where credit is due. Dr. Allison deserves every dime I have given her, every dime. And the woman isn't cheap.

"That's been coming for awhile, hasn't it?" Wren say. She's so close, an inch or

two from my ear. "Are you done with me? Am I being dismissed?"

I put a finger to my lips, hoping she will shush. Wood stairs are just beyond the metal cot, though deep in the shadows. I start to climb the steps but I only get to the fourth one before my head bumps into closed cellar doors. I raise my arms above my head and push them as hard as I can manage. The wood doors are locked from the outside.

@wren&me1 In the end there is only what I think, feel and see. I tell that 2 myself as a way of telling it 2 Wren. Does she mind me growing up?

NINTEEN

THE CELLAR DOORS are behind the house. This is a narrow backyard that goes on longer than I would have guessed. It's very weedy, very unkempt. Islands of thigh-high grass and brush grow amid an expanse of dirt and tiny stones turned silver by the moonlight. It's still a dark early morning. The sky is cloudless and has enough stars to light this shabby backyard and show me where I need to go. Toward the end of the yard is a windowless Tudor-styled shed the size of a one car garage. It's probably a tool shed or maybe a place to store the usual junk, rotted canvas lawn furniture, Christmas decorations that would embarrass Jesus, etcetera, etcetera. But who's to say that one of those items in there isn't Carlos, Jr.

"Why don't you just call the police," Wren says.

This made up dialog between Wren and I has always felt like comfort food. It's very soothing to pretend I'm not alone, that I have a friend who will come to my defense. But she's changing. How many times have I said that lately? Little things. For example in the last ten or so minutes her accent has become less British and more American, more like my talk.

"I *al*ready called the police." I can hear my exasperation.

"Please don't do this, lovey."

"I don't see a choice."

What am I going to do, walk off and abandon my

child? Who does that sort of shit? Perhaps Carlos, Jr. won't be in the shed. That could be the Good News or the Bad news, depending on where and how soon I'd find him. Perhaps Mother calls and says my son is asleep in the front seat of her Lexus and why don't I get myself home and give him a big hug – the one call I wouldn't mind getting.

IT'S TOO SMALL in here, the outside and the inside are not the same. I think the outside of the shed is actually bigger than the inside. By half or more, I don't know. And I don't know what such a thing would mean. But that's how it seems, anyway. A strong smell of lavender saturates the air. It's a disinfectant, not a perfume. The interior is immaculate, the concrete floor buffed and without a blemish. Sheets of polished metal pegboard cover the walls. Tools are fitted to the pegboards in précised rows – four down, six across. A tan wood worktable goes the length of the right wall. And it doesn't simply look clean, it looks new. The tools look new, too. Something isn't right but at this point my paranoia is rampant and I don't trust my perceptions. Maybe Edward takes very good care of his things, many men do. They'll sweep the floor and wash it down. They'll label everything and scrub their worktables. Men do that all the time.

"Or he doesn't use any of it," Wren says.

"Why have tools and a shed you don't use?"

"...for show."

Yes, okay. That's what I think, too.

This is when I see Edward's cane on the worktable. A florescent lamp is above the table, suspended from the ceiling, the light reflecting off the gold handle. I reach for the cane but stop.

"Afraid to touch it?" I hear Wren's sarcasm right away. Tonight I feel she is examining my words, my actions.

"I'm...cautious. Let's leave it at that."

"Oh yes. A very excellent place to leave it." Her

mood has shifted to something lighter. Laughter, vague and distant. "You be cautious, lovey. That's you, that's what you do."

"You like me feeling this way."

"We can't forget old times."

"Things change," I whisper.

"...not all things."

I am afraid to touch Edward's cane and I'm embarrassed by my fear. Why did he leave the cane on his worktable? I don't know, maybe a man who needs a cane might have more than one. A spare; we have spares for everything, why not a spare cane? There is also an opposing argument: a man who uses a cane but doesn't need one would leave his cane anywhere.

THE THUMP AGAINST the back wall is sudden and audible enough to startle me and I take a quick step back. There's a second thump followed by a third. The tools on the metal pegboard quiver. I want to call out, *Is that you, Carlos?* But I don't know who or what's doing the thumping and me becoming a frantic mother could very well make the situation worse. I study the wall, reaching toward it, touching the wall with my fingertips. Another part of the shed's interior must be hidden, that's what I'm thinking. That's why the inside of the shed appears smaller than the outside of it. I tap as lightly as I can on the metal pegboard, my hand moving across the wall. Another thump. Someone or something is answering me.

"...hello?" I said it very quietly then press my ear to the wall.

It's like braille, isn't it? Moving my fingertips over a pegboard. But I don't know the language and all the notches in the boards are the same. Meaning alludes me. Still, I believe the grooves and the notches will speak. That the wall itself will open and reveal its secrets.

"YOU'RE A VERY greedy little girl," Edward says.

"Shut up, you sick asshole."

"And a real mouth."

Carlos, Jr. is strapped to the cot next to me, wrists and ankles secured to the metal headboard and footboard. He's been gagged, too.

"I'll be taking my boy."

"First you want Michael, now you want this one, too." Edward is standing a few feet from me – no cane and no hint of needing one – his voice calm and even. "This is unacceptable. You want my nephew, that's okay. I'm tired of Michael. He's doesn't appreciate a roof over his head or a warm meal. But you don't stop there, that's you're problem. Michael isn't good enough for you. You want this one, too. This skinny one, you want them both. Is that what I'm hearing, deary? Because if that's not what I'm hearing, please tell me. Please, speak up now. I'm a fair man, I want to be fair."

Then Edward says I won't be leaving here and I say I'm the one with the pistol.

And unless he has a bigger pistol, Carlos, Jr. and I will be leaving here faster than he can fucking blink. I tell him this as I'm unbuckling the leather restraints on my son's wrists and ankles. He has bruises where the leather was too tight on his skin. The army cot is like the one in Edward's basement. But there's no blanket and the gray mattress smells of urine. A strip of duct tape covers the boy's mouth. I keep Mother's pistol pointed at Edward as I peel the tape, my glances shifting between the two of them.

"Are you hurt?" I say to Carlos, Jr. I am nervous and don't give him a chance to answer. "Did he touch you? Did he do anything?"

"...I'm okay."

"You don't look okay." I have a thumb and forefinger on his chin and I turn his face left and right to see if he has anymore bruises. He looks normal, I suppose. "It's going to be fine," I say. "I'm not letting you down, Carlos. Not this time, Mommy promises."

"I want to go home."

"C'mon, baby. See if you can stand up."

The room is lighted in dull purple and there are posters of boys on the walls, all of them Carlos, Jr.'s age or younger. Blond boys and boys with dark hair – an all American look – everyone well-scrubbed and white. Some boys with their shirts off, some wearing jockey's, some naked. Caucasian is obviously the race of choice for Edward. A big wall to ceiling wood cabinet is behind him. The double doors are open and I don't know the names of everything. Whips, I know. Ropes, handcuffs, harnesses, those sorts of things.

There are black latex and leather clothing hung in an orderly way on metal hooks. I also see hunting and surgical gear. Knives, mostly. Every item has its place and each row is an equal distance from the next one. Special locations for special things, it's very much like the tools on the pegboards.

"Must you go?" Edward says. He's wearing pressed jeans and one of those short sleeve pullovers that has a collar, what's called a golf shirt. His white hair is slicked back and he doesn't look as puny as the night I saw him watching TV in his bathrobe. Edward isn't a muscular guy – certainly not that – but he's tall and he doesn't seem bothered that

I have a firearm pointed at him. "Let me fix you something," he says, all friendly, the perfect host. "I'll scramble us a few eggs, a slice or two of bacon – an early breakfast for you and your cutie here. I'm absolutely starved, aren't you, deary?"

"WHAT WAS THE cane? An affectation?"

"More of a rule," Edward says.

I'm holding Carlos, Jr.'s arm and helping him get up from the cot. We are still in this hideous room with its dull purple light and the posters of those children on the walls, those boys. Edward is keeping his distance but I know if I lose my concentration for just a second he will be on me and do his best to take the gun.

He's talking about the cane and why he uses it. "...the rule is, 'Appear less than what you are.' It's a wonderful rule, if you think about it. Simple but elegant." He takes a step forward and I bet he doesn't suspect I see him do it. Then Edward says, "I learned this from Vincent Gigante, not that I knew the man personally. You remember Vincent?

They called him The Chin, Vincent the Chin. He worked for the Genovese family. I forget when, the nineties, I think. Vincent used to wander around Greenwich Village in an old tattered bathrobe. People would say, 'Look, there goes crazy Vincent.' But he wasn't so crazy. Or maybe crazy like a fox – more that. Crazy like a fox. 'Appear less that what you are,' it's a good lesson." Edward grins at me, his teeth are long, even and white. "Now how about those eggs? You and the cutie want some eggs?"

I'm kneeling in front of Carlos, Jr. and tucking his t-shirt into the waistband of his khakis. My pistol is still aimed at Edward and I'm looking at the man as I talk to my son. "I want you out of here." I say this to my son. "You understand, Carlos? You run. You get out of here now."

"I don't know," Edward says. He shakes his head, an exaggerated doubtfulness. Mr. Concern. "What is it? Two-thirty, maybe three in the morning? It might as well be midnight it's so gosh awful dark. And a bad neighborhood at that. It's not a good place for a boy to be alone, is it? Nicetown, what a name. Don't you simply *love* the name? Above average crime rate –

murder, robbery. Nicetown. Go figure."

"Better than here," I tell him.

"That hurts my feelings." Edward's voice is even and calm. "Okay? All right? If you want the truth, my feelings are hurt. First you steal my precious nephew. My dear brother's only son, a boy I love as if he were my own flesh and blood. But a burden, I'm not a rich man. The boy is difficult and a financial burden, I'll be very honest. If I am anything, I'm an honest man." Edward is brushing an invisible something from the knee of his jeans as he talks, lint or something. He's saying, "...*then* I attempt to teach you about your actions and their consequences. Here I am – an older, wiser man – I could have been someone's mentor. But what do you do, deary? You go and hurt my feelings. It's unbelievable. Who does that, what person of good taste?"

"I'll meet you home okay?" I say this to Carlos and I shove a twenty dollar bill in his pocket and turn him toward the open wall panel that leads to the phony-baloney tools shed. "Go on. *Now*. Do it, Carlos, *go!*"

My son is off and running. A moment later I hear the shed door slam shut behind him. After that I don't hear anything at all.

HE'S ON ME in the snap of a finger, it's that quick. My eyes had flicked away from Edward to watch my son as he was leaving this awful room – the urine smell, the purple light, those sad posters – I only wanted to see my boy run out the shed door and escape this horror. And Edward was on me. I just didn't think, that's the long and the short of it. But if Carlos, Jr. is free, I don't care about the rest. Let my baby be safe and grow old– *run, Carlos, you keep running* – and let that be that.

Edward is faster and stronger than I thought. In

our first encounter I'd come from behind him in his living room and used the chloroform. That was nothing like tonight. I hadn't given him the chance to show his stuff.

He's straddling my chest now, his left hand gripping me by the hair, his right hand pressing the barrel of Mother's pistol against my forehead. It's bad enough if he shoots me but to get shot with my own mother's pistol, I don't know, it's depressing.

"What to do, what to do," he says, a sing-song voice.

"Get the fuck off me."

"No profanity, little girl." He hits me hard above my left eye with the gun barrel.

Pain flares into the center of my brain. Things get black with bits of silver and I'm on the edge of consciousness. *Stop it*, I think. *Don't you faint. Don't give him the satisfaction.* And I hear Edward say, "We won't have that sort of language. Not here, none of that in my presence. That's *not* how ladies talk to gentlemen."

"...I'm hurt. You really hurt..." I can't get my words out.

"No, no, no, *no*," Edward says. And slaps my cheek once, twice. "No fainting allowed. C'mon, c'mon. Eyes open. Bright-eyed and Bushy-tailed. Let me see those pretty eyes, that's my girl. Big smile. Can you give me a smile?"

"...you're...crazy..."

I'm pretty sure I pass out because there is blood on my lip and I don't remember being hit. Edward is still sitting on my chest like some schoolyard bully. There is a hum or buzz to the purple colored lights. Along with the urine smell, there's also something new, an odor of garlic. It's coming from Edward. It's not so much his breath as it is his body odor. I feel my stomach start to cramp and nausea burns its way to the back of my throat.

"I can't let you to leave," Edward says, very matter-of-factly. The barrel of the pistol hasn't moved; I feel it against my forehead. "I hope you see the obvious – you going to the police, making a fuss, the TV news. And please don't tell me how you'd *never* do that and how I *ought* to trust you. Yada, yada, how boring. No, I can't let you leave. Most people in my position don't clean up after themselves, that's the number one problem. Details. Everything must be professional. Everything, the "T"s crossed, the "I"s dotted. "

I start to panic. *This guy's really going to kill me.* I feel my skin go hot and cold at the same time. I feel it on the back of my neck and on my face. "Please, I'm a mother. I mean who's going to take care of my son?" I hear myself pleading. I'm using my son to save my life. I feel guilty and humiliated but that doesn't stop me. "Who is going to take care of Carlos, Jr. Please, listen to me. I have a mother and she doesn't have a clue about kids."

"You won't be alone, deary." Edward says. "After killing you, I will also kill myself."

"...what?"

"Prison life doesn't interest me."

"But what about Michael?" I'm grasping for anything. Believe me, not being the *only* dead person doesn't make me feel any better. "You have an obligation. I mean you and I have responsibilities, don't we? Our children depend on us."

"Don't you worry," he says. It's that sweet sing-song voice. "I'll get rid of the boy posters and such, the lights, the paraphernalia. We will look like Romeo and Juliet, you and I. Lovers who made a pact and died together. It'll be very romantic, you'll see."

"That's sounds very nice, Edward. You've thought

a lot about this, I can tell." I'm trying to keep it together; keep it calm, casual, how I want to present myself. I am the reasonable argument, the one he's decided to ignore. But inside I'm very close to screaming. "We must put aside our personal interests and think about Michael. What will become of him without your help?"

"I don't care." It's a petulant tone, a man who hasn't gotten his way.

"Of course you do." My skin is cold and wet with sweat and I want to climb out of this skin and run away in my muscles and bones and fine my son. God the pain in my head won't quit, it's terrible. "Sacrifices are required, aren't they? For our children. Isn't that what we say? Surely you must see that."

"He's not a grateful boy." Edward has placed the barrel of the pistol to my right temple. He studies this for a moment or two before returning the barrel to its original position against my forehead. The man is figuring out the best spot to shoot me. "I feed the boy, I give him a place to sleep, I buy him gifts – and what do I get? Do I get a thank you, a hug, a kiss of appreciation? Some token of his affection? No, no, I get nothing for my efforts, my devotion. He finds me repulsive."

"But he's a child."

"He eats my food, doesn't he? He stays in my home. Many boys don't have a home. Many boys are in orphanages. Do you think these orphanages are concerned with the welfare of children? All they care about is the money, their paychecks." Edward is becoming more and more angry as he talks. "This is my baby brother's child. I've opened my heart and home to this boy and I get nothing."

"Perhaps you want more than he can give you," I say.

"Let him be on his own. Let him rot in hell."

Edward jerks my head sideways, still holding my hair. He has decided to shoot me in the right temple.

I am out of things to say. I glance about the small room, the purple light and the shadows, hoping to see Wren. My Wren. I want comfort from her voice, I want her guidance. She's always been there, but I don't see or hear her. *This isn't the time to say good-bye*, I think. *It's no time to leave a friend*

"...Don't do this...please," I tell Edward.

"You're lucky," he says. The barrel of the pistol dig into my temple. "This is a quick death. Do you know how many people *long* for a quick death? One-two-three, it's over? Hundreds, probably thousands. People dying of cancer, people in constant pain, people who are caught in their depressions, they'd be envious of you. 'Why am I not lucky like her,' they'd say. 'Why is life so unfair.' Believe me, deary, suffering is endless."

"...don't."

I shut my eyes. I can't quit shaking, my shoulders, my legs. And I've pissed on myself, I know it. Edward probably thinks it's the stink of the mattress but the smell is definitely coming from me. I'm also waiting for the click of the trigger but I don't hear anything. Seconds pass and nothing. Finally I peek at Edward and he's struggling with the pistol but it won't fire. For a very brief instant I want to apologize and tell him it's my mother's pistol and what can a person expect. But then I hear something that sounds like the backfire of a car, maybe louder. Immediately I feel stings on my left cheek as if a bunch of hot angry bees had just attacked. Edward squeals and grabs his left leg with both hands and rolls off me.

My cheek is aching. I tap at the wound gently, the raw jagged skin. And I touch my fingertips to my tongue and taste the blood.

Michael is standing at the entrance to the open wall panel and he has the shotgun his father used for duck hunting, the one in the cabinet by the TV. The heel of the wood buttstock is still against his shoulder, ready to use again. Fluorescent lights from the tool room on the other side of the open panel give him a luminous outline. Near the door to the shed I also see Carlos, Jr. Once more he's a boy who refuses to take my direction but tonight I am glad. He's waving his arms over his head and smiling.

I walk across the room, my legs unsteady. Everything is either numb or hurts like hell. I take the shotgun from Michael and both boys circle their arms around my waist. It's a good feeling. We are relieved to see each other, that's for sure. I glance about the room for Wren as if she might show herself, my ever constant witness, ready to judge my performance, to tally up a grade, her vague presence forever in the shadows. But it's just me and the boys tonight and that's more than enough. That's just fine.

@rwaye&son 1 day at a time. Learning 2 keep Wren in the books & Carlos, Jr. in my heart. It's a better Waye. ☺

EPILOGUE

IN MY DREAM, I am walking in the desert. Probably it's the Sinai, though who knows for sure. Why do people live here? That's what I'm thinking. The sun is too bright and too hot and I can barely see. Along with lots of sand there are rocks and some low brush but no shade, no relief. I feel heat coming through the bottoms of my shoes. Once in awhile a breeze will turn the sand – whirling it, a little funnel – and it stings my face and neck. It's early in the afternoon, the sun directly above me, the sky a vivid pale blue and without a cloud. This is a timeless place, an endless discomfort.

I'm looking for my father.

"CARLOS, JR. AND I are going back to Chicago." I tell this to Dr. Allison after discussing my night with Edward and how my son and I almost got ourselves killed. My left cheek is bandaged where stray buckshot hit me, a proof that speaks for itself. I'm watching her for some type of reaction. Of course Dr. Allison is writing in her notebook but she does shake her head in disbelief when I describe Edward putting Mother's pistol to my head. Then I tell her, "The man's in the city jail, thank God." And I smile. It's a nervous sort of smile that's gone before it has a chance to make itself known. "The judge didn't grant bail. One of the cops told me Edward is too big a risk, so he's there 'til the trial."

Dr. Allison is wearing her gray suit with a beige silk blouse. Her short hair curves about her ears, not a strand out of place. She always has that fresh unruffled look. Her style is much like the style of her office, both understated and mysterious. Empty white walls, indirect lighting, a temperature that's never too hot, never too cool, the office and the occupier are interchangeable.

"Mother wants me to stay with her," I say. I am sitting across from the doctor in one of the twin tan leather chairs. "But you can't stay with your parents and be an adult, or I can't. I'd regress in a heartbeat. And it's not that Mother's a bad person. I mean she's a little self-absorbed but aren't we all. No, this is about my son, it's about Carlos. His friends are in Chicago, things are familiar. I haven't been thinking about him and I need to do that, I *want* to do that. He's my life, my boy."

WHEN I SEE him I will want to call out his name but I don't know what to call him. He was never a real father and J.D. sounds too personal. A hot gust of sand whips about me and I cover my eyes and nose until the wind settles itself. In the dream I think

I have walked for miles and miles but the sun is staying in one place and won't go along with the day. Hand to brow, I squint and try to block the light. I see three, maybe four yards in front of me and that's it. Still, I have not come this distance to give up. He's here and I'll find him and I'll watch him die.

"...AND MICHAEL?"

"What about him?" I hear my defensiveness.

Dr. Allison doesn't answer me. It's my cue to "say what comes to mind," her favorite expression. *So what comes to mind, Rhea. What are your feelings, what are your thoughts.* Too many of both, if I'm honest. I'm feeling overwhelmed. Right now the court has allowed Michael to stay with The Little Sisters of Mercy. This morning I got a call from Sister Kathrin who wanted to know how I'd feel about being Michael's foster parent. "It's not like adopting, you know," she'd said and tried some humor, "It more like renting." I think things are happening too fast. I love Michael, and I wanted him far away from Edward. But does that mean he's now my son?

"I'm scared," I say to Dr. Allison.

"Uh-huh, tell me about that."

"One boy is a lot for me. Two, I don't know."

"Is that a decision you have to make today?"

See she has that way about her. It's such a throwaway sentence but said at the right moment it can straighten your world – or *my* world. I don't have do everything today, this very second, Dr. Allison is right. Michael can come visit us; we can get to know one another. Six months, less. Who knows what will happen. Don't get me wrong, impulsive is nice. Let's go to the beach. Let's have pizza. But the important choices require time and thought.

A SHADOW GOES over me. It stops the sunlight for less than a second; then it's gone. I look toward the clear sky, my hands half-cupped about my squinting eyes like invisible binoculars. What I see is one of those big hideous birds. The ones with the scarlet faces and the white beaks and the wide black wings. And it's doing what it did in the stories Mother used to tell me about my father and his time in the desert, the stories I'd draw as a little girl. This dark bird is gliding high above me, circling on the current. The sun is too strong to watch it for long. The bird circles a final time before it sets course and begins flying ahead of me but in the direction I've been walking. At that moment I know I'm on the right path.

"WHEN DO YOU leave?" Dr. Allison wants to know.

"A couple of weeks. Carlos, Jr. has school." I glance down at my folded hands in my lap and I smile. "He's really misses his friends."

It's a comfortable room, I never thought I'd feel this way here but I do – a secure sort of feeling, so difficult to explain. But I've grown to appreciate everything about it. I like the vague cinnamon scent of Dr. Allison's perfume. I can't believe I'm saying this but there's even comfort in watching her write notes.

"You look deep in thought."

"...I think Wren is gone." I'm surprised by the words.

I get no comment from the doctor, nothing. It's another way she has of saying, *Tell me more.* Or, *Go on with your thoughts.* She has a hundred ways of doing that. I used to find it insulting and hurtful. But there is a freedom in knowing I can say what I want, whenever I want. Occasionally it's almost too much freedom. Is there such a thing?

"...I feel empty," I say.

"I can imagine."

"Why? Why can you imagine?"

Dr. Allison places the cap back on her pen and closes the leather notebook. Her talk is careful, slow, considering her thoughts. Maybe she plays things in her mind before saying them out loud.

"...a father who was never there," she says. "And a Mother who was devastated by the loss – a very depressed mother is my guess. 'Unavailable,' that's the word I need to use." She leans toward me slightly, her elbows on the knees of her gray slacks. "Why wouldn't you feel empty now? Wren was what filled you up, wasn't she?"

"...will she come back?" I feel anxious about both choices.

"I don't know." Dr. Allison gets up from her chair and lays the notebook on the edge of her desk. This is what she does when my time is done. And she says, "Wren's absence tells us you're stronger. Does that make sense to you?"

"...yes."

THE BIRDS ARE gathered in a circle. Wind drives the sand around them. They appear and disappear. But the heat and the brilliance of the sun does not quit. At first I don't hear anything but wind. Then I hear a wet sound, the tug and pop of flesh. I clap my hands and yell, "Get out! Go on, out of here!" And I clap my hands again. Wide black wings spread and push downward and the sand and the gray dust becomes a storm. The birds rise and force themselves toward a clear sky and sunlight. They do not scream or cry. The only noise is the pull of their enormous wings.

And what do they leave me? In my dream, in the bits of bleached out clothing, fragments of a tan shirt, decayed scraps of khaki, what offering is mine? No blood,

no flesh, nothing shows a recent life or any life at all. Though briefly I do think this isn't true. There is a skeleton and certainly that belonged to a life. But it's the color of sand and rock. And as the wind beats at the day, parts of the skeleton begin to splinter, a chin, a forehead, an arm, chunks of the thing. I'm watching it break apart, little piece by little piece; and I know when the wind is finished, I will have no proof, not even bones.

❄ ❄ ❄

Thank you for reading.
Please review this book. Reviews help others find
New Pulp Press and inspire us to keep providing these
marvelous tales.

If you would like to be put on our email list to
receive updates on new releases, contests, and
promotions, please go to NewPulpPress.com and sign
up.

ABOUT THE AUTHOR

Ron Savage has published seven novels, a story collection – two more novels and another collection on the way -- and over a hundred and twenty-five stories worldwide. He has both a BA and MA in psychology and a doctorate in counseling, all from the College of William and Mary. Ron has worked primarily as a therapist. He has also worked as a newspaper editor, actor and broadcaster.

www.newpulppress.com

www.ingramcontent.com/pod-product-compliance
Lightning Source LLC
Chambersburg PA
CBHW070457260626
47161CB00004B/1342